A Small Fairytale

By Judith Duke

PAGE PUBLISHING, INC.
New York, NY

First originally published by Page Publishing, Inc. 2017

ISBN 978-1-64082-346-4 (Paperback)
ISBN 978-1-64082-347-1 (Digital)

Printed in the United States of America

CHAPTER 1

B rutally beaten and raped, she lay barely conscious.

She had been delayed leaving work, coming out an hour late into the quick darkness of early spring. She ran, shrugging her slender shoulders into her coat and turning the comer in time to see the diesel exhaust of her bus as it pulled away from the curb. She made a little sound of dismay as she looked around.

The same waning light was turning the alleyways into darken lairs.

Not that she was alarmed. For all the lack of attention given her by the city, she had never thought of it as unsafe or even uncaring. She had a good, if ordinary, job; a small apartment; and the exhilarating chance to plan her own life.

Now the departure of her bus rendered the immediate future a little problematic. She had money enough for a taxi, but there was none in sight. The night breeze tossed her banner of dark curls about, and she shivered suddenly. She glanced around and saw the brightly lit hospital less than a block away. She decided to go and wait there for a taxi or a later bus.

She teetered on the curb waiting for the light change, for although there was no traffic, she was an obedient girl and awaited the signal.

With no warning, not even a half heard footstep, she was seized by her hair, and she fell into the nightmare. Dragged behind the empty building, she was flung to the ground. His hands were all over her then, tearing away her clothing, exposing her body to the night and to him. She felt the first incredible pain as he drove himself into her body, and she arched and went rigid. With brutal force, he continued the violation, and winded by pain, she could not cry out even if there had been anyone to hear and there was no one.

This was another world, unimaginable, that silenced the outside one and magnified the sounds of her hell. His sour breath muttered curses and little jeering laughs as he thrust again and again. His weight crushed her almost to suffocation as he pinched and tore at her whole body. Sneers fell with his sweat and he laughed again and spat in her face. The spittle fell into her open mouth and although she gagged and retched, the foulness slid down her throat, and she knew she would never be clean again.

She felt his hand beneath her blouse again and his sharp nails closed on her breast, twisting the nipple and tearing the flesh from aureole to armpit. She felt the separate sting of the cold spring air the length of the wound. Sometime later she became aware of the same coldness between her legs and realized he was lifting his weight from her. She lay shattered without moving, knowing somehow the act was not complete.

He stumbled about her, slobbering ribald giggles then leaned over and, with a hand in her hair, dragged her to her feet. He hit her with open hand and clenched fist until he tired and then he threw her to the curb and began kicking her with a heavy booted foot. In a fading move toward self-preservation, she rolled to her side, covering her head as best she could with her torn arms and bringing her knees up. In the last few minutes of her awareness, he stepped back, cursed again then his heavy boot made contact with her temple, and she at last lost consciousness.

The person who found her quite literally stumbled upon her, his foot sliding on her hair. The jerk of her head brought forth a moan, and he fell to his knees feeling for the source of that cry. He searched about, still startled and already apprehensive of what he would discover. Inadvertently, his hand touched her exposed breast so he knew a woman lay there. The broken cry had sounded like "No! Ah, no!" to him, a heartbreaking sound that set his teeth on edge. He reached higher and touched her face and felt out the savagery wrought there. He fumbled in his jacket for his penlight. The brilliant, tight beam threw her features into sharp relief, showing her face paper white while blood flowed sluggishly from her cheek and mouth. Her clothing was torn, and there was blood streaming faintly in the night air everywhere he looked.

He snapped off the light and very carefully felt out her shape and lifted her into his arms. Her head lolled back across his arm, and her body was a deadweight against him. She made no sound now, and bending close, he could not hear her breathe so he feared her dead.

He moved quickly out of the shadows into the faint light reflecting from the storefront and held his burden like an offering toward the glass. For a moment, he stared at her throat, at last seeing the faint pulse. He was a doctor and he turned toward the big hospital now, bearing her swiftly and easily. Her blood was on his hands and clothing. In the glow of the Emergency Room sign, he could see her throat and shoulders already blackening and the bruises from coarse hands were everywhere he looked.

Inside the hospital, he eased her onto the stretcher that came with practiced speed at his call. The great clinical compassion already moving in quick response. Under the merciless lights, she lay crumpled and exposed, and he felt a quick pity for her defenselessness. Nurses and technicians were immediately about her, violating her body again from medical necessity. She moved beneath their hands, beginning to awaken. Her head tossed so that the pillow was stained on either side of her tom face. As she awoke further, her hands flew up, and she pushed desperately at the faces bending over her. He reached out, caught her flailing hands, and held them until the nurse could secure the restraints. He felt her terror in his hold. She was not yet fully conscious and in such shock; he doubted she knew her surroundings, but he must be free to work.

The doctors on duty had joined him. They moved about her in an organized drill evaluating and examining as the nurses attached their many machines. The girl on the table drifted in and out of consciousness, crying out and subsiding. In the way of hospitals, she had become a situation to be dealt with, an incident to be resolved in their best manner. At that moment, she was only a broken body to be repaired. Whatever any of them felt for her was translated into impersonal competence and medical brilliance. They worked on ignoring the pathetic moans in an effort to stop the downward spiral of shock.

A small flurry and Hergert, a gynecologist, arrived. They made room for him, and he bent over her, moving her legs apart. Her agitation increased, and she cried aloud in protest. A quick look, and they were moving her toward the surgery, a group of them like runners about her bed.

In the operating room, she lay draped, her body sectioned into medical arenas, her dirty curls hidden by the theater cap. Capped and gowned himself, her rescuer nodded to the anesthesiologist. Then as he reached to turn her head slightly, she opened her eyes and looked directly at him. For a moment, she stared then; her eyes clouded and she began to struggle.

The anesthesiologist made a move toward her, but suddenly one of her hands came free and flew up to catch her rescuer's hands, still about her head. Her hand closed tightly like a child's upon his gloved thumb, and she stared at him again with that clear blue intensity. Then abruptly she yielded to the drug and slept. After a moment, he eased her hand back into the restraints and the surgery began.

He saw her only once again before leaving the hospital. She still slept sedated as he bent over her. Her lacerated face had swollen her eyes shut, and her shoulders and breasts were black above the tight white bandages encasing her broken ribs.

A tear inward from her armpit had left a pattern like a falling comet, ending in a deep star shape at her nipple. It seemed likely she would always bear that mark, but he would not see her again.

He had already been leaving the hospital for a year's sabbatical when he found her; and now, many hours later, still wearing her blood on his clothes, he left her case with other doctors and was gone.

CHAPTER 2

She became conscious of someone calling again and again: "Jennifer, Jennifer!"

Who was Jennifer? She ignored the voice and drifted away again. Still later, she heard the voice again but she knew no Jennifer, and she had sensed the savage pain awaiting her. She floated out of its reach and slept again.

The next time the summons were so insistent she acknowledged its authority and came to it. As she had known it would, the pain seized her so that "Not Jennifer, Jenny" came as a cry that tore her cracked lips.

"Jenny, then," the voice continued. "Jenny, how are you feeling?"

After a moment, she touched her lips carefully with just the tip of her tongue. Immediately something cold and moist touched her mouth with extreme gentleness so that tears of gratitude gathered beneath her shut lids and spilled onto her face. She turned her face, questing, and the touch came again. A tiny trickle ran down her throat, and she swallowed audibly.

"Jenny?"

"I hurt," she said piteously. And the pain rose in waves, sweeping up from her feet, bursting white hot into her groin, spreading out to scald her whole body. There was no strength or resistance in her anywhere, and she lay limply like some small forest hoping the fire would top out and spare her but feeling the furnace of pain rising again. She swallowed dryly, and this time the trickle of water was a little longer.

"Jenny, I know you hurt. There's someone here who needs to ask you just a few questions. Can you answer now?"

Her mind shied away, preoccupied with the pain, not yet remembering why she hurt, only that she did. At last, just as they thought to rouse her again, she made a small motion of assent.

A new voice spoke, overloud but moderating immediately at her fretful grimace.

"Ms. Dexter, Jenny, did you see the man?"

The man? What man? Did I see the man? Oh god! Oh god, oh god, oh god! No, no, no, no! Her head began to turn restlessly on the pillow and her hands fluttered in agitation.

"No. No. No!"

"Ms. Dexter, I must ask you. Did you see the man? Can you tell us anything?"

"No! It was dark! No, I didn't see him! I couldn't see him! No, I didn't, I didn't! Her eyes flew open. "Don't you know, I didn't know he was there!"

The first voice of the nurse came back again and firm hands caught Jenny's gently. Cool hands that had held the water touched her hair lightly, bidding her stillness.

"Rest, Jenny. We know you didn't know he was there. He shouldn't have been there. It's all right. It's all right." But Jenny knew it would never be all right again.

Later of course they came to question her again. But she could tell them nothing more. It had been dark, she had missed her bus, and before she could cross the street to where the lights were, he had seemingly risen out of the ground to attack her. She had seen no more than his shadow.

"Were you a virgin, Ms. Dexter? Not are you, but were you?"

"Yes, I was a virgin."

"Do you have a family we can notify, Ms. Dexter?"

"No, there was no one."

"Do you have some place to go, Jenny? Will you be all right?"

"Oh, yes, of course." There would be some place although she could never go back to her apartment. She fumbled with the clasp of her purse. He had not wanted her money for drugs or her credit card. But what if somehow he had seen her name, her address?

She was in the hospital a long time, but when at last she was released, she was reluctant to leave its refuge. The world outside, once so bright, looked gray; and there were shadows everywhere.

CHAPTER 3

There were the nightmares, of course.

They had begun even in the hospital, and she had known to expect them to continue. But in hospital there was always someone to awaken her, to turn on the lights, and to sooth her. Now the horror continued unchecked until her own sounds awakened her. Sweating and shaking, she would run to cling to the toilet, retching streams of bile. She showered until the boiling water ran cold over her crouched form; she scrubbed the scar on her breast until the flesh was raw, but it healed anew each time without diminishing until at last she accepted its permanence, like a brand.

A deep distrust of the world itself entered her soul. It did not seem possible that something so terrible could have happened in a world she had found so beckoning; a world that had seemed as full of delicious possibilities as a candy store. Now everything was overshadowed, veneered with an ugliness she had known existed but had never had contact with. She understood perfectly now the meaning of a phrase she had heard once in church: "the stain of sin." Surely not her sin? But the stain was indelibly over her whole world now.

In her new apartment, she had a compulsion to check the many locks repeatedly. She would lie down only to fly up in a panic convinced she had overlooked one, stumbling in her haste to reach the door in time. The smallest unfamiliar sound was a heart-stopping jolt.

She had changed apartments immediately, leaving no forwarding address, just taken her belongings and gone. Those same belongings lay in heaps where she had dropped them. It seemed to take more effort, more concentration than she was capable of to see to their arrangements. Sometimes she forgot what she was searching for in their midst and wandered away empty-handed, careless of the confusion. She went for days when she forgot to eat and nights she dared not sleep.

She managed to keep her job in the impersonal secretarial pool where she had worked for more than two years largely unnoticed. Her immediate supervisor had been informed; her co-workers believed an automobile accident explained her long absence and, on her return, offered sympathy and turned back to their work. She was not unpopular but had always been a bit reserved in the midst of the suggestive office chatter and gossip and had not made real friends. The tides of their lives swept on, eddying easily past her small overly quiet self.

She was sensible to the fact her rapist held her captive still by her fear, but she could find no escape: her reason was no match for her fear and revulsion.

She fought panic daily, not only the panic of the nights, but panic that assailed her by day surrounded by her fellow human beings, caused indeed by those same people.

The touch of another person became intolerable. Even the brush of a passing shoulder in the close office left her nauseous and shaking. The appearance of a male coworker brought the cold sweat beading on her brow and her hands clenched tight enough to leave the imprint of her nails. Although she knew her inclusive fear of all men to be irrational, the fear grew into real terror and she stood her ground by sheer force of will.

The gynecologist who had attended her urged her to receive counseling.

She had gone to one meeting of the rape crisis group but had been so horrified at hearing expressed aloud all the feelings she strove so to suppress, she had fled and had never gone back. Catching a glimpse of herself in a mirror one day, she saw the reflection of a gaunt, pinched face with soul sick eyes and recognized it as her own. Overly thin with the once bountiful gay splurge of curls scraped back painfully, there was no trace of the girl who had once worn such hair, who had run toward life with quiet joy, whose delicate being was one of true beauty. That girl had died at her attacker's hand, and the reflected girl looked to be dying also.

The thought did not distress her, rather it afforded her her first consolation.

CHAPTER 4

At the end of the fourth month, she realized she was pregnant.
It seemed impossible in light of such overwhelming physical ravaging. And certainly the hospital had routinely done everything possible to preclude such an outcome. But somehow the tenacious little life had begun and had held on.

She did not return to Dr. Hergert. Driving the old Volkswagen she had bought when she could no longer endure the press of public transportation, she went across town to a public clinic. The doctor there, a woman, seemed strangely hesitant after the examination, looking at Jenny with quiet eyes before confirming her pregnancy. She helped Jenny sit up, and her hand rested a moment on her shoulder.

"Do you want to continue this pregnancy, Jenny?" she asked, and Jenny understood the compassion in the other woman's face.

"I think I have to," she said at last, reaching for her clothes.

She didn't know how she had come to that decision, for the first hint of pregnancy had filled her with such disgust she had felt she would convulse. She had lain shuddering thinking of the spittle that had gone down her throat as if it were the cause. Her first thought then was to rid herself as quickly as possible of the abomination. She felt she could take the knife herself and split her body apart to seek it out and remove it like a cancerous growth. She had raged with the first show of spirit she had exhibited, vowing this would go no further. She would not bring forth the monster bred on her body. She would kill it in the womb, strangle it with her very hatred; she would withdraw her blood from its parasitic nourishing so that it withered and died like a shriveled fruit. Her body jerked as though she would

13

shake its dead form free, and on her breasts, her nipples folded in upon themselves, denying suckle.

But somewhere, someway, the hot righteous hatred faded and like a whisper, thoughts of the baby began to fill her heart. She conceived a great pity for it, for its innocence, for the underserved hatred it bore yet unborn, and for its helplessness. She yearned to protect it from any knowledge of its beginnings and to stand between it and the world, which had so harmed her. There was no longer any thought of destroying this life but only a rising dedication to its birth and well-being. The thought of the child filled her mind as its development swelled her body until his imagined tiny face, his cap of shining hair like a fluffy yellow chrysanthemum, his little starfish hands with such incredible little nails, his searching mouth and baby wail became as familiar to her as if she held him in her arms. The first flutter of life lit her dreaming face and her fingers felt light, magical, as she touched her belly over his little form. The tears came with her thankfulness for this treasure and she vowed again to protect him always.

She felt sure she carried a son and the thought did not trouble her.

She would look upon his maleness without dismay and know him to be no monster, not part of one, but a child she would raise to be the man all men should be.

She threw herself into cleaning and organizing her apartment, making a home now of rooms she had barely noticed. She began to care for herself, preparing wholesome meals and eating regularly, taking long walks in the fall air and swallowing her vitamins so that she regained health and a look of vitality. And it was all for the baby. In her sleep, her arms would curve as though she held him to her breast. His fuzzy teddy bear smiled from her pillow in the soft nights.

CHAPTER 5

∽✺∽

W hen the baby died at the end of her sixth month, she knew she would have to find some way to follow him for there could be no life for her ever again.

There had been no warning. His heartbeat had sounded strong and sturdy as a little boy's should at the clinic the day before. She had imagined him turning with that little flip that delighted her so to burrow into her side, nestling beneath her heart to fall asleep, secure in her love and protection. She had touched her hand over his head and smiled, soothing him with gentle strokes of her fingers. He had stilled under her touch, and it was the last time she ever felt him move.

When it was all over and the storm of grief and regret and denial had raged to the edges of sanity, she began her plans to die. Above all, she wanted to die somewhere in such a manner that her body would never be touched again. Save for that one thought she would have returned to the street corner where she had already lost her life and let death overtake her there.

The mechanics of arranging to die took what strength she had left. She had no gun, could get no drug, and despising herself for a coward knew she would never be able to cut her wrists. Nor would she end her life by another's hand. At last, she overheard an evening weather report and looked up to see the deep snow that had fallen and was falling in the mountains. It lay thick over the dark earth, and she imagined herself crawling beneath its cover, hidden from the world, and giving herself up to whatever lay after death, if anything. If there were a God who had somehow overlooked her while watching the sparrows, then her son would be there; if not, so be it. There could be no greater suffering awaiting her; she bore the ultimate now.

In the end, she went very quietly. She packed away the few papers and letters she would keep from prying eyes, closed her apartment, and drove out of the city toward the mountains in a steady snow that looked to strengthen.

Many hours later, her little car at last refused a snowdrift and shuddered to a stop. She had seen no one for miles and judged herself so far into the wilderness as to never be found. That was all she wanted—all there was left to want. The snow was falling quite heavily now. Soon she and the car would vanish without leaving a trace in the white silence.

She unfastened the seat belt from around the baby bear and wrapped him in his blue blanket. Outside the car, the frigid wind lifted her hair from her shoulders, and she tucked the bear deep inside her jacket. She struggled up a rise toward a big fir tree half seen through the swirl of snow. She lifted the heavy trailing snow-laden limbs and crept beneath and lay down. Her footsteps were already gone. She rested her cheek on the drifted snow without feeling the cold. Her breath made little white wisps that came slower while the last of her tears fell into ice unheeded. Only once she stirred and brought the bear to her lips, cradling his head with a smile for in her dream she held her baby at last.

CHAPTER 6

The dog was overjoyed with his discovery. He raced down the slope, running in circles around the man, urging him back toward the line of trees. The man accustomed to the dog's exuberance only smiled and lifted an admonishing hand.

"Let's go, Max. Time to call it a day."

The big dog paused, looking at him with bright impatience then he bounded a step or two away and back again, whining and barking eagerly.

"No, Max. Let's go, boy!"

The man began to move away from the copse of trees. The dog tried another bark then raced back up the hill, plunged under the low branches of a fir, snatched something, and then made another pass around the man and dropped a woolen cap at his feet.

Ignoring the startled exclamation, he was up and under the tree again, pawing and whining with joy when St. Agnes joined him, showering snow over them both as he made his way under the branches.

The girl lying there looked unreal. Her hair was frosted and frozen tears glittered on her pale cheeks. One hand was outstretched and the dog began washing it as St. Agnes fell to his knees, gathering her into his arms. She came so easily, was so infinitesimal; he was hardly sure she was real. The dog appeared to have no doubt and leaped up to nuzzle her face, causing the doctor to stagger as he stood.

"Whoa, Max! Good boy, great job!"

The dog swerved away satisfied and ready now to show the man their familiar way home. St. Agnes followed the dog's lead, his head bent to the girl in his arms.

He put his cheek to her mouth, seeking her breath, and then buried his face in her throat, willing his warmth into her. There was no response at all, and the pulse beneath his thumb was a fluttering that might stop at any moment. The short distance to the cabin seemed beyond attaining. Briefly in the back of his mind ran a quickly forgotten thought of having carried someone like this before with the same urgency.

They reached the steps at last, crossed the porch, and burst into the warmth. Max ran to the hearth and settled himself by the fire as St. Agnes laid his too still burden on the closest settee.

He wasted no time but set the water running in the big tub and then began stripping away her stiffened clothing. She had been completely inadequate dressed and her smooth flesh was cold as the marble it resembled. He worked quickly desperately; unaware of beseeching mixture of prayer and profanity he had begun.

When she was naked, he hurried her into the bath and, supporting her head on one arm, began rubbing her arms, her legs, her body, trying to bring them warmth. Her hair floated over his arm, the last of the snowflakes dissolving.

When at last a little color began to show in her skin, he lifted her out, wrapping her in a bath sheet, and laid her again on the couch as he renewed the cooling water. Beginning at her feet, he rubbed warmth toward her heart, striving to stir her sluggish circulation.

Max came to stand at her head, whining encouragement to St. Agnes whose distress he felt.

He took her again to the tub, testing the temperature with his bare arm as he had discarded his upper clothing. He began again, his face close to hers, talking to her, urging her to feel the life he was chafing into her; to fight with him for her life. Her face was closed and still upon his arm. He could see no expression at all, but he sensed here complacency and grew angry with her indifference and with his helplessness to stir her to the struggle. His voice alternately chided and coaxed.

After a long time, he felt her move just a bit beneath his hands, and then she drew a long shuddering breath. Her pulse steadied, and he knew he had won the first battle.

He lifted her from the water for the last time, wrapped her in a soft blanket warmed sometime by the fire, and sat down with her on his arm. He was exhausted, the sweat sheening on his body. As he reached with a towel to dry her hair, the blanket slipped from her shoulder. He moved to gather her closer. The loose blanket slipped again, and then with a start, he was cupping her slight breast, staring at the little scar, and recognizing in spent amazement just who she was.

CHAPTER 7

Without awakening, she fell into a natural sleep. She was faintly flushed, and her pulse continued strong, but he doubted she would escape so easily the effects of exposure. How long she had lain there in the bitter cold, he had no way of knowing, but he knew she would not have survived much longer. Max had been her savior. He glanced at the dog settled now before the fire as if he knew that for the moment the crisis was past. *Thank God for Max*, he thought, as he looked back down on the girl in his arms.

He was worn out from the hours of exertion and anxiety, and he stood up and carried her to the bed where he cocooned her deep into the blankets. He lay down beside her, his hand on her wrist, and was instantly asleep.

He was awakened several hours later by Max's lick on the back of his neck. He looked over his shoulder to see the big dog with both front paws on the edge of the high bed, looking apologetic, needing to be let out. The doctor in him turned back immediately to look into the face of the girl whose wrist he still held. The reassuring color still held.

He let Max out and watched him gambol off in search of fresh adventure. A weak sun shone but more snow waited behind it.

He built up the fire, went down into the cellar, and checked the furnace as he always did and brought up another armload of wood for the fireplace. The cabin was his second home, built for the time he would spend long periods of solitude, retreating to continuing his medical writings. A cabin needed a fireplace, but he didn't want to be dependent on one, hence the furnace.

With no phone to interrupt him and with a well-stocked larder and freezer, he was self-sufficient and content. He had not expected to leave the mountain until late spring, and yesterday's snowstorm guaranteed that. They were on their own now.

Although he had left her for only a short time, he went at once to the bed.

After a moment, he reached for a chair and sat down at her side. She lay deeply asleep with her lashes dark on her flushed cheeks. She looked very fragile, as if made of porcelain, breakable. He reached out a hand and brushed her silky hair from her brow. Her mouth drew down the least bit at the contact, and he immediately moved his hand away. He searched her face then with his eyes, seeing the faint scars from her beating that would eventually fade completely. His colleague, Bethesda, had done a good job there. He hoped Hergert had been able to do as well. The line of her face was sweet; she looked delicate, dainty, untouched.

But he remembered all too well the bloody, grimed, and swollen face he had first seen: torn, streaked with tears, and blackened with bruises. Fury flared in him as it had that night and was as quickly concealed beneath his calm, but he knew he never would have recognized her without the scar on her breast.

Max barked at the door, and he went to let him in, glancing again at the pale morning sun. The hospital and all its equipment was far, far away. He filled Max's bowl with dog chow and replenished his water bowl as his mind catalogued the medicines he had with him.

He prepared his breakfast and made coffee, crossing often to the bed where she slept on without moving. He shared his toast with Max and then prepared a thin gruel and kept it warming. When he had cleared away, he got out his stethoscope, warmed it in his hand, and laid it to her chest. She sighed but didn't rouse, and after a moment, he continued his examination. The flush on her cheeks was more pronounced, and her breathing was growing quick and shallow. Her temperature was obviously rising. He would make an attempt to feed her some of the broth. She was going to need all the strength they could summon.

He brought the bowl, a towel, and the softest shirt he could find in his clothing. He turned back the blankets, seeing the growing effort of her breathing in the rapid rise and fall of her breasts. Her back was altogether too warm to his touch as he maneuvered her into his shirt, buttoning it down the front and rolling the sleeves. It came to her knees and afforded her a little modesty. He eased her back against the pillows and let her rest awhile. Then, the broth was "just right." He lifted her up and tucked the towel like a bib around her.

She fretted the first touch of the spoon and then scowled fiercely so that in spite of his worry, he smiled. He persisted, however, urging her with little touches and tastes, until at last she accepted a few swallows. The effort seemed to further exhaust her. She made a small fluttering move with one hand, turning her head away with resolution and sleeping again without ever having opened her eyes. He set the bowl aside and eased the pillows from her back.

"Sleep then, little one. I'll be here."

CHAPTER 8

T hen as her pulse had occupied him during the night, so now did the sound of her breaths. From frigid cold, her body had taken fire, burning with fever as congestion filled her lungs. He stood over her with a syringe, but her bared arm looked so pathetically childish he turned her to inject the antibiotic into her hip. As gentle as he was, she cried out at the small sting, and he felt an overwhelming pity. What had she ever known at a man's hand save pain?

Through the long hours, he tended her, using all his abilities and resources to carry her through. Twice a day came the injections, and each time she cried out a little so that he approached with dread what he must do. Once in a late afternoon when he turned back the quilt, she seemed to anticipate his intent, and she sobbed aloud though she made no move.

Her labored breathing tightened his own chest until he felt he took each breath with her. He thought again longingly of the hospital and recognized the futility of the idea. Live or die, it depended solely on him. And he did not intend to let her die.

Again, he had the feeling he fought alone. She was far too passive, far too willing to let the fever take her, as if she rallied against her will. He leaned over and looked at her, lifting her into his arms to ease her breaths, trying to call her to him, to extract her promise to help him. Her chest labored with each intake and the hectic color stained her cheeks, but she refused to regain consciousness. She lay limply, divorced from the struggle, leaving it all to him. The nights came and passed, bringing more snow. Max was his constant companion, always at his side, offering the comfort he seemed to know the man needed.

At times St. Agnes despaired but the hours passed and still she lived, an unwilling captive of his determination. The fever rose to an alarming pitch. He slid his arms down her back seeking to ease her position. She had wakened and began to struggle, expending her small strength in agitation: an agitation that grew frantic and gasping while her body went rigid. Realizing he was the cause of her distress, he moved away until her thrashing ceased; and then slowly and easily, he drew her hands into his and began to sing very softly an old lullaby he only half remembered. For a moment she pushed wildly at his hands and then she quieted as he sang on, improvising when he forgot a word. She lay at peace as long as he sang, and her breath seemed to come easier, so he sang the lullaby as if to a small sick child, and she responded to the warmth of his voice.

The torment of her body and mind over the past months had left her dangerously fragile. She was ill for many days, unaware of anything beyond her own world of pain and fevered dreams. Her temperature rose again and again as he fought the pneumonia that fed it. He bathed and sponged her with easy hands that veiled his concern, seeming to see the very flesh dissolving, burning away as she grew weaker.

When the chills came, he wrapped her feet in warmed cloths, bundled all the covers about her and held her close, warming her with his own body heat. He fed her, coaxing her swallow by swallow, and held the cup to her lips. When she grew delirious, moaning and pushing frenziedly at his hands, refusing to let him touch her, he sang the little lullaby until she subsided and accepted even his most intimate care. He snatched what rest he could at her side, his hand always touching her as he slept with her against his chest. The slightest move, an uneven breath, and he was bending over her with concern.

The signs of recovery came slowly. Had not his overzealous sister insisted he pack a plethora of medications, there would have been no recovery at all. The few times he thought she would waken, she seemed to retreat. Once in tending her, he moved suddenly, preventing a spill, and she drew up her knees, flinching away, trying to shield herself from the danger she perceived. She stifled an outcry with bitten lips, and he stood back until she relaxed in sleep. He continued his care with a schooled face that belied the furious pity it concealed.

At last, one midnight he awoke to find her awake, her fever stated, gazing into his face with calm intentness. He lay perfectly still by her side, almost afraid to breathe as she searched his face feature by feature. She looked up suddenly to meet his look. He saw fear shock her eyes wide then her look traveled frantically about the room. She frowned a little, her thrust moved as if she would speak, and then she sighed and her lashes swept down.

He lay awake a long time after that, thinking of the terror he had seen in her eyes, felt in her body, and knew a time was coming when it must be dealt with. He knew from the moment he had recognized her she had come to the mountain to die, and from that same moment, he had made a vow she would not succeed. He looked down at her sleeping now curled against his side. His arm had come about her as always, and as always in her sleep, she lost her fear and seemed to take comfort in his touch.

"Don't worry, little one. We'll make it through," he whispered. "Sleep and grow strong," On the edge of sleep himself, he realized he had no idea of her name.

CHAPTER 9

After many slow days of recovery, Jenny woke. She was alone in the big bed and lay perplexed but not anxious, lassitude denying all but the mildest of curiosity. Something had awakened her and her eyes searched the room languidly. All was quiet. She could hear only the lazy crackling of the fire. She frowned a little, weak with a fatigue too great to do more than gaze about. Slowly she took in the room; the high oversized bed in which she lay warmly secured in soft bedding, the quilt tucked right up to her chin; an armoire in which she saw several items of clothing, not hers, hanging, and a tall bookcase crammed neatly with an overabundance of books and journals. A small table was by her side and an assortment of items lay tidily there by the lamp.

The folding doors of the room were open, and she could see easily into the main part of the house. To her right was a large airy office with big windows behind an oversized desk that was overflowing with papers and books around the latest of computers, and some sort of manuscript evidently in progress. *That desk is a mess*, she thought, but that was the only sign of untidiness anywhere. All else was in order.

On the other side of the bed was a door that presumably led to a bathroom. In front of her just outside opened a large living area with more bookcases, just as crammed, and a large couch, a settee, and several chairs. A rocking chair was by the fireplace and next to the hearth was a cushioned window seat. She could see nothing out the windows but mountains and trees. Her gaze came back to the room. Scattered rugs broke the gleam of the fire on the oak floor and a large oval rug was under the chairs near a kitchen, which ended the room. There were paintings and photos she could not make out from where she lay. An afghan or two and brass and candles all brought warmness to the room. She rested quietly, recognizing a haven although she did not remember why she had need of a haven. Her gaze swept the room again as she turned her head into the pillow, losing interest.

A bark roused her to look through the windows by the door where she saw a large gray dog prancing in the deep snow, looking toward the house where someone she could not see evidently stood. Who? She heard the sound of a voice mildly admonishing the dog and her heart jerked. Why? Real panic assailed her, but she fought it down, refusing to yield to the terror she could remember no basis for. She could see the man now as he stepped just off the porch. He stood with his back to her, his hands thrust in the back pockets of his jeans, bareheaded despite the cold, the sun striking his light hair. He was broad shouldered and fit, and he moved with grace as he bent now, scooping up a battered Frisbee, which he flung to the dog. He was laughing as he turned, and she saw his face, vitally alive, attractive, and familiar.

She knew this man, then, somewhere but how? Bits of memory came to her, bits of pain, but this man had not caused any of it she was certain. But there had been pain, deep pain, more than she could ever think of. She shut her mind down frantically and lay panting, overcome with the fear of remembering. As she heard the door began to open, she was seized with fresh terror even as her mind refused to lay its cause to this man. She closed her eyes, feigning sleep, seeking to regulate her breathing.

Immediately when he entered the room, he went to the fire and warmed his hands and then crossed to the bed and took her hand easily into his, feeling her pulse. He touched her brow, brushing back a tendril of tousled hair, and then laid his fingers at the base of the throat against the heartbeat he felt there. He seemed not quite satisfied, and she felt him looking down at her for what seemed an interminable time before he moved away from the bed, and she risked a glance after him. The fear jerked again in every nerve of her body, and she felt poised to take flight, even as fatigue began to protest her taut muscles.

He had gone to the stove and soon the fragrance of a substantial breakfast with coffee wafted to her. She felt a faint hunger. The dog came in, was warned from her bed, and threw himself with a thump before the fire. The man took out plates, dropped some utensil, and swore mildly. The dog yawned, got up again, and shambled to his bowl; knocking a chair with another thump, gradually the small routine sounds soothed her so she unclenched her hands and lay back among the pillows, her speeding heart calming.

At the stove, St. Agnes prepared an invalid's breakfast of toast and oatmeal with his own breakfast. As soon as he had approached the bed, some tension, some quality of her breathing told him she was only feigning sleep although she did it well. She had shrunk the least bit from his touch, but secretively, not openly resisting him as she had in delirium. He wondered how much she remembered and felt a great sadness that she must remember at all what had sent her fleeing from life. He was nagged by the idea of something more, something worse than even the rape and beating if that were possible. Something that had overcome her courage and begged her suicide.

Although he had seen no movement from the bed, he felt her panic and began softly to whistle and then the sing the foolish lullaby. It was a sweet song and made the room seem safe and warm. He made up a tray and left it to keep warm at the back of the stove. Moving easily and still whistling softly so she would know his whereabouts, he took his coffee and moved to a chair some distance from the bed. He sat down facing her, and as he did, a memory came to mind.

Once as a boy, he had found a young fox in his father's barn. It had been hunted and hounded, run to death, and it had made its way into the warmth to hide, to die. He had been struck with a horrible pity for the creature and sickened by the fear in its eyes. He had approached it with extreme caution, making one small advance after another until it had suffered his presence, and he was able to help it. In a few weeks' time, it would come to him at the end of his school day as joyously as he to it. Now he was ready to bring into play all he had learned of wild things to the wounded creature he had found in these woods.

He sat for a while drinking his coffee and watching her, dreading the moment he must further alarm her, knowing nothing was going to be easy from now on.

"Are you awake now, little one? If you are, I think it's time you tried a little breakfast. Then perhaps we can talk a little."

She didn't answer, but he heard the swift intake of her breath.

He rose and brought her tray to the bedside. When he looked at her, her eyes were open, wary, and unblinking like the little fox's, but not looking away.

"It's all right," he said. "I'm not going to hurt you. Let me help you to sit up to eat."

He slid his hands carefully behind her back, making no sudden movement, letting her see his intention each time before he touched her. He could feel the tension of her body and the slight shrinking, but he let him raise her and she accepted from his hand the little she managed to eat. She sipped the weak tea with his hands supporting hers on the cup, and then she lay back spent.

Again, he eased her into comfort and she slept a little, hearing in her sleep the homey sounds of his clearing up in the kitchen.

In the early afternoon, she began to stir, and he came to sit by the bed recognizing her need before she came awake. When she did awaken, he gave her no time for embarrassment.

"Do you need to go to the bathroom now?

The blue, blue eyes showed a trace of gratitude as she nodded. She moved as if to rise, her gesture revealing her weakness.

"No," he said again. "No, you must let me help you."

He ignored the sweep of color into her pale face and lifted her, folding her to himself with familiar ease from the many days of care. In a few minutes, he came to carry her back to bed, still allowing no embarrassment.

She turned her head into the pillow as he tucked her in; and then, sounding thoroughly exhausted, she spoke at last: a low, unused-sounding voice, "Who are you?"

But she slept before he could reply.

CHAPTER 10

S he woke again late that evening, bewildered again and only half remembering the day. It was as if her mind and body were too worn to allow her more than snatches of reality. She knew she had been ill, was still ill, and that she was tired. She moved her hand slowly along the quilt, looking out the window into the snowy night. The fire murmured in the next room, a little lamp by her bed held back the shadows and the dog had crept in to lie on her rug. Now at her movement, he looked up at her so entreatingly. She put out a hand, and he stretched up to nuzzle her fingers. She stroked his broad head, rubbing his ears, and he leaned nearer, offering to join her on the high bed. He looked so huge she shook her head with a little smile.

"No, dog," she whispered.

St. Agnes laid down the book he had been reading by the fire while she slept and crossed to her bed. Max seemed all too ready to ignore her refusal.

"No, Max," he echoed firmly, and the dog dropped down disappointed but obedient. St. Agnes patted his head. "Good fellow. But she's not ready yet to play with you."

She leaned back on the pillows, turning her head to look up at him as if she were summoning the courage to do so, a strangely defenseless movement that made him aware just how vulnerable she was. Her eyes were wide, not afraid, but near. He stood perfectly still, giving her time then moved to sit by the bed with the dog at his knee.

"Hello," he said with a smile.

She didn't speak for a moment. He saw her mouth quiver and then steady, a betrayal not only of her fear but of her unsteady courage.

"Hello." Her voice was so clear that now he could hear the fear quite easily.

"How are you feeling?"

Again the little hesitation, then, "My head hurts, and my chest."

At dire note in her voice, Max moved to touch her hand as St. Agnes wanted to. She acknowledged the dog with a little pat but still watched the man.

"I'll give you something for your head and then you must let me listen to your chest". He had not moved, but he saw her small recoil and her immediately recovery.

"All right," came almost in a whisper.

He rose without hurry and brought the tablets and a tumbler of cold, cold water. Letting her lead the way, he help her to sit up to drink. He reached then for his stethoscope waiting on her. She nodded after a minute and lay back against the pillows. He counted the pulse leaping beneath his fingers and then reached to put the stethoscope to her chest.

As he touched her shirt, she shivered as if she couldn't help herself and then allowed his hand.

"It's all right, little one. Just take a deep breath for me. That's a good girl. Deep breath and another. OK, good girl. Lie back now."

He was not entirely satisfied with what he heard in her lungs, but he would not subject her to a more thorough examination now. He stood back, frowning a little without realizing he was, and his face was remote, forbidding. He glanced up to catch her expression and his own gentled.

"Your head should be better soon," he promised.

"Who are you?" she countered.

He laughed a little. "Yes, we need names, don't we? I can't go on calling you 'little one' forever. Can you tell me your name?"

She frowned in puzzlement.

"Jenny."

"Jenny," gently. "Very nice. No, I didn't know," he answered her look.

"Why?" She stopped to steady her voice. "Why am I here? I've been ill, haven't I?"

Here it was then. He went carefully, not knowing what she remembered, not wanting to tell her anything.

"Yes, Jenny. You've been very ill. But you're getting better every day although you're still weak."

"But if I'm ill…? Why am I here? Are you a doctor?"

"Yes, I'm a doctor."

"But why aren't I in a hospital? Why am I here?" she persisted, almost beneath her breath. He waited without speaking, reluctant to answer her, unable to think of a way to explain without further alarming her.

"How did I get here? How…?" she began in rising agitation. "Did you…? How did…? No! I don't want to remember!" Sensing hovering horror, her eyes filling with tears, met his. "I don't have to remember yet, do I? Not yet, do I?"

"No, Jenny. You don't have to remember. Don't worry!" Inadequate words, he knew.

Her hands flew to her face, closing in fists over her eyes, but the tears found their way around.

"When, when must I remember? When do I have to remember?"

"When you're ready to remember, Jenny, not until then." His voice hardened. "Or never!" he said.

"I'm so afraid of you," she whispered.

"I know you are, Jenny."

She was crying openly now in wild weary little sobs that took his breath. He sat down on the other side of the bed without touching her, though he longed to hold her.

"Jenny, listen to me. You've been very ill, and you're not at all strong now. You don't need to think of anything you don't want to think of. Just let it go and don't worry about it. Let me help you get well. I know you're afraid of me, but I'd never hurt you. Turn over now and talk to me. Come now, don't cry anymore."

Under the spell of his voice, she turned, gradually calming. Her hand fluttered like a bird seeking shelter. He held out his own hand and hers came into it. She was exhausted, still shaken by shudders, but in spite of her fear, she recognized his touch to bring comfort, and she clung to his hand.

After a while, she said again, "What is your name?"

He laughed a little; she sounded like peevish child.

"For my sins," he said, "it's St. Agnes. Theodore St. Agnes."

She smiled sleepily, the first he had seen. Her drowsy eyes searched his quiet face. The lamp gilded his light hair. Once she had dreamed of hair that color, but she couldn't remember why.

"Did your mother call you Teddy?" She was nearly asleep, her voice growing husky.

A memory of his mother, dead a year, fell like a gift into his mind. Oh, yes, she had, usually in admonishment with laughter lifting the edges.

He laughed himself.

"Well, she didn't call me Saint."

CHAPTER 11

There followed quiet days of rest in which she began to regain her strength. She slept most of the mornings and again after lunch, deeply asleep, breathing so quietly he went over to the bed to reassure himself. He stood for long moments, his eyes sweeping her face, lingering on her features until satisfied all was well. Her appetite improved and her color came back. She spoke very little but submitted to his examinations though not willingly at least without dissent. Her head bowed to her bended knees, she suffered the stethoscope to her bared back. Only once did her hand come up as if to stay him. He was intent on a persistent rasp in her lungs, but he caught her gesture. He smiled and straightened, moved her pillows down and left her to sleep again.

Each time she roused, her eyes sought him out as if, like the little fox, she had need to orient herself in relation to him. He saw this and was very careful not to startle or alarm her. As she began to sleep less, he found her eyes on him every time he glanced up and saw the effort it took her to control her fear. He had reason again to be thankful for Max's presence. He kept up a running commentary to the dog, and the sound of his conversing seemed to lull her. Max was by her side each time she stirred, and often, he saw her lean down to bury her face in the half-wolf's thick ruff.

Near the end of a fortnight, he decided after lunch one day she needed a change of scenery and drew a chair to the fireplace. He established her there, wrapped in a blanket, while he changed the bed again and fluffed up the pillows. As he did, he saw her look thoughtfully around the big cabin and laughed a little to himself. No, little

Jenny, only one bed but big enough we can share. By now, she had to realize they had been sharing the bed for many days.

She wasn't ready to lie back down, so he offered her a couple of books which she thumbed through listlessly. She leaned over to rub Max's ears, holding back the tangled weight of her hair. He left her with the dog as he carried the bed linens to the basement to be washed. He could hear the low sound of her voice murmuring to Max and was satisfied she was all right while he was downstairs.

The few pieces of her own clothing, washed and folded, were there in a cupboard, with the bear and his blanket He picked up the toy, wishing he was not certain what it told him. There were too many little clues, and the time frame fit all too well. He wished with all his heart it were not so. He feared the time she would remember; knowing there would be no easy way through, only praying there would be a way through. He tucked the bear back in the blanket and closed the cupboard.

She was still restless when he went back upstairs. He suggested and ran a bath for her. When she had discarded her single garment and wrapped herself in a towel, he came to lift her into the big tub and helped her wash her hair. Then he left her to bathe, and when she was finished, he returned to help her up and hand her another of his shirts warmed by the fire.

There had been long moments of silence, the water stilled as she sat in the bath. Now as she sat wrapped in a blanket on a cushion by the fire while he toweled and combed her hair, she was very quiet. Her shadowed eyes searched the snowy landscape outside the windows as though only now fully realizing their isolation, and she shivered so that he asked quickly if she were cold. She shook her head no, and he didn't question her further. Her hair was long and as the short winter day ended and the night drew in, he sat lifting and combing the long length of her curls until her hair was dry. Her bare feet showing under the edge of the blanket worried him, and he rose to bring a pair of his socks. She accepted them and leaned down to pull them on, running her hand along the sleeve of his shirt as she sat up, as if conscious she wore nothing at all of her own. Panic touched her, and then he saw curiosity. Several times he saw her hand come up as if to touch her scarred breast then drop.

She ate her supper, brushed her teeth, and turned her face into the pillow. She suffered his ever anxious ear to her chest and answered his "Sleep well, Jenny" with a subdued "Good night" of her own as he laid his stethoscope aside.

He turned Max out for a run and stood with his shoulder against the comer post, watching the moonlight on his river below. The dog plunged about, raising the scent of some small animal and running in eccentric loops while St. Agnes waited.

When he came in, he gathered his own necessities and took a long shower as if he too had troubling thoughts he would wash away. Then in the pajama bottoms—he had never worn before Jenny came—and barefoot, he sat trying to read but images of her, bloodied and beaten, kept filling his mind. He finally gave up on any attempt to read or to listen to the radio he kept turned to a whisper. He was restless and almost certain Jenny was not asleep. He made coffee and drank it, built up the fire for its company, and watched the bed without seeming to until he thought her asleep at last. He screened the fire then, turned off the lamp, and went to the bed. He realized she was not asleep as soon as he lay down, and he drew his pillow behind his head and waited.

"Teddy?"

So it was to be Teddy, not Theo or even Ted, but his mother's choice. The thought came to him how much his mother would have loved this brave girl.

"Yes, Jenny?"

"I was raped, wasn't I?"

"Yes, Jenny, you were." He thought her voice entirely too controlled.

"I remembered when I saw the scar. In the bath, I mean. I don't really remember though. Somehow I know it happened, but I can't really remember."

She lay with her face turned away. The moonlight revealed the curve of her cheek, the sweep of her lashes. Her expression was remote.

"Do you know how it happened?" she asked almost politely.

"No, Jenny. I left the hospital to come here the same night just a few hours after we brought you out of surgery. I don't know."

She turned to him, startled.

"Were you there then?" Her voice was wondering.

"Jenny…" He laid his hand on the sheet between them, and in a moment, her hand came into his. "Jenny, I found you and brought you to the hospital. I was with you in surgery with Dr. Hergert and Dr. Bethesda. I saw you afterwards in post-op for a few minutes before I left."

"But you found me? Where was I? Why were you there?"

"I was at the hospital checking on a child I had had in surgery earlier in the day. I was turning the case over to another doctor, and I wanted to go over everything again before I left. I was on the way to my truck, parked there near the bus stop, when I found you. You were there just in the alley." It took an effort to keep his tone even.

"Did you…Did you see anyone? Was anyone there?"

"No, Jenny, only you." In spite of himself, his voice grew harsh. "And I thought you were dead."

"I thought he would kill me. I hoped he would. I remembered thinking that. It's funny," she said in a tone he found not funny at all, "I can remember parts of it, but it's as if it were something I read about. I can't feel it."

She lay quietly for a few moments, her hand still in his.

"But how did I get here? Did you bring me here? Why have I been so ill? Teddy, I don't understand."

The "Teddy" had the power to enslave him, he thought on another level. "You've had pneumonia, Jenny. And you weren't really over…the time in the hospital. That's why I'm so insistent on keeping a close watch on you now. No, I didn't bring you here. I, rather Max, found you in the woods…Jenny, do you not remember at all coming here?"

"Coming here? Why would I come here? I just remember pieces of things. I can't make any sense of it!" She touched the shirt over her breast as he had seen her do during the evening. "I remembered the rape when I saw the scar. I remember trying to scrub it off and the blood, but it was always still there. It will always be there, won't it?"

"'Yes, Jenny. It is how I knew you."

He had answered what she had asked him, but he would not volunteer details. He couldn't risk a relapse in her weakened condition. And there was much, very much, he did not actually know.

She was silent for a long time, and he lay watching the expressions chase across her face. Puzzlement, loathing, horror, and finally fear; such fear he felt disgust for the whole human race.

"Jenny," he said when he could bear her look no longer. She started violently, and her hand jerked from his.

"Jenny," he said again quietly. "Please don't be afraid. I'm here to protect you, never to harm you. You're lying here now with me. You've slept in my arms all these nights, and I have done nothing more than try to make you well. Try to sleep now and rest knowing you're safe. I won't hurt you, and you can be sure no one else will either, even again."

Her eyes were enormous in her tired face. She stared at him until at last, her lashes fell, rose and fell again and she slept.

CHAPTER 12

She walked a tightrope between terror and trust. At times he knew she feared him desperately. Trembling, with clenched fists, she forced herself to stand her ground and allow his voice to soothe her to stillness. At other times, she turned to him quite naturally. He never knew what evoked which response, but knowing the strain she was under, he did not expect reasonableness. He saluted her shaky composure.

She had remembered little more and what she did remember held no emotion. It was yet as if it had all happened to someone else: horrible and regrettable, but something she was able to look at dispassionately. How long this would go on he had no way of guessing. The little toy bear made him more certain she had been with child and had lost her baby. If so, this was completely blocked, and she made no reference at all to the savage beating she had survived.

Only once in this period of relative calm did he see a forceful reaction.

She was standing beside him in the kitchen, waiting for him to hand down a bowl from an overhead cabinet. He was busy with something on the stove and said absently, "Just a minute, sugar," without even hearing what he said, much as he would have spoken to his sister or one of his nieces. But she didn't answer and the quality of her silence came sharply to him.

He turned to find her white-faced, clutching the cabinet for support. The next moment she was running to the bathroom, retching into the toilet by the time he reached her. He knelt beside her, holding her head until the spasms passed. Then he drew her into his arms there on the bathroom floor and held her as she sobbed.

"That's what he called me, over and over and over again. 'Sugar,' 'Sugar,'" she whispered in shame, her hot face in his throat.

She shrank from remembering and at the same time despised herself as a coward for her lack of recall. She drew out what details she could from his knowledge: details he gave once, unwillingly, and refusing to speculate further with her.

"It will come when it will come, little one. And hurt when it does come. Leave it!"

But she could not. She worried it in her mind, turning and tearing at it, repelled but resolute. He wished to God she would leave it alone. He always knew when she thought too long or came to near remembering. Then in spite of herself, she startled at every move he made and drew back as he passed her. In turn, he despised himself for frightening her, not realizing that at times it took no more than the look of power of his hands, the play of muscles in his shoulders, or the faint shadow of his beard: quick reminders of his maleness to being on the panic. When he saw what she could not hide, he ease with small talk. He would put aside what he was doing and take Max for a long run along the river, leaving her alone to recover herself.

In the long evenings while she prepared for bed, he went to his desk and worked on the articles he would present at a series of medical conferences in the spring. He worked purposefully late, but often when he came to the bed, she was still awake. Insomnia began to alternate with restless sleep, and often it was near morning before she slept soundly. When he found her awake, he sat by the bed talking until she drowsed. If she were asleep, he lay listening to her quiet breathing until he too slept. In the nights somehow they drew near each other, and although he never grew accustomed to finding her in his arms each morning, he came to expect it. His arms would tightened for a moment, then he would ease her from him without waking her, brush back her hair to see her face, and as always lay his fingers to her throat to touch her pulse.

It was inevitable remembrance would come.

He found her one midnight sitting on her heels in the middle of the high bed, staring out the dark windows behind the bed, the angle of her body drawn tight with tension.

"Jenny?"

She couldn't answer without losing control, and she shook her head blindly. When he leaned over her, bent on picking her up, she took hold of his shirt with both hands and his cheek came down to her tear-streaked face. He could feel her trembling, her slight figure shuddering.

"Teddy, please…!"

His arms closed about her, and he lifted her from the bed. Like a child, she buried her face in his shoulder and the sobs broke free.

"Oh, Teddy! It's all coming back, and I can't stop it. I wanted to remember just a little and a little and get used to it, but I can't stop it. I can't stop it! Oh, I was so afraid, so afraid, and it hurt so much. And I tried, really I tried, but I couldn't get away. And he hurt me and he hit me and he…"

Here her voice fell to an agonized whisper so that he bent his head, his hand on her nape, holding her cheek to his to listen. He would hear it all, every word, as if by hearing he could take her burden for himself.

"He told me he would—me—and that I was a whore—and he hurt me. He hurt me!"

Her voice gasped and shook, whispering the vile words she couldn't say aloud, and so shamed he could hardly listen, as sickened by her shame as he was by the filth she had endured. As the horrible little story unfolded, he felt he could bear no more, but he held her to him and listened without interruption. Her words came in a moan, her head tossing on his shoulder so that her hair came into his mouth: that same hair he had seen matted with her blood.

"Teddy! I'm not what he said I was. I've—I'd never been with any man!"

The tormented little change of tense did not escape him.

"No, Jenny! Of course, you're not. And you've not been with a man yet!" But she was too distraught to take his meaning.

"He called me filthy, filthy names, and said he would—" Her sobs choked her until she gasped for breath. "Teddy, Teddy! I couldn't get away! He was so heavy, and he held my arms behind my back, and he hit me so hard! My face was bleeding and I couldn't move it and all the time he was, he was—I tried." Her voice was a wail. "Teddy, I tried! But I couldn't get away!"

"Jenny, I know you tried. There's no way you could have gotten away. It wasn't your fault, baby. None of it was your fault!"

"And Teddy, when he—finished, when he—he hit me over and over again in the face. When I fell, he kicked me and called me that name again until he couldn't see where I was to kick me, and he stepped on my hand, and then he kicked my face again and I fainted. Oh, Teddy! Why did he do it? Why? Why?"

But she was crying too hard to have heard his answer, if he had had one. He could only hold her, wanting to weep with her and knowing more pain lay ahead.

At last, she began to quiet. He held her without speaking, and she lay against him, feeling the strong sure beat of his heart. His hand was in her hair, soothing her tangled curls from her wet face, drawing her close.

After a time, he lifted her face. The intuition was strong in his mind.

"What else do you remember, Jenny?"

She began to weep again quietly. He picked her up and walked with her in his arms to the window where he stood looking down at the river that had brought him to this place, at the cold clear moonlight striking the water far out in the middle where the current ran too fast to freeze.

"Tell me, Jenny," he insisted quietly at last.

It came in whispers and in broken phrases choked with sadness and longing. The terrifying discovery she was pregnant, her rage against the unborn child followed by her overwhelming love for it: a love born of her compassion for its need, a love that denied the horror of its conception, a love that gave the child reality long before its expected birth.

"Teddy, his name was Christopher. I knew he was a little boy, and I loved him so much."

They were seated now by the fire, and he rocked her as though she were the baby they spoke of.

"I knew just how he looked, how he would look when he was big enough to walk and play. He had blond hair, and his eyes were so blue. I could see him in his little red overalls, running to me and laughing.

"The clinic doctor asked me if I wanted an abortion and I thought I did at first, Teddy. She thought the baby would always remind me of—but I never saw—his face. And I never knew my parents, so if he hadn't looked like me, he could have looked like them. But it didn't matter! I loved him, and he was my son."

Her voice broke.

"Teddy, he was my little son!"

He let her cry, her face buried in his throat, her tears wetting his shirt, and thought of her little boy. The child's face seemed to live in his own mind: a sturdy little boy who was not to be.

CHAPTER 13

S he was quiet the next few days. He brought upstairs the little
bear with its blanket and gave it to her without a word as she sat
chin to knees in the window seat looking down at the river. She took
the bundle with a grave look as though asking permission to grieve,
and then she turned the bear into her arms and held it close. For a
long time, she didn't move, but he saw her tears falling on the little
blanket. After a time, he came to her and she leaned against him, still
watching the river, still crying silently.

Hours later, the tears dried on her cheeks, she lay beside him,
her face shadowed by the firelight in the next room.

"It was all my fault, Teddy. All of it. My fault for being there
after dark. If I hadn't been late, it never would have happened. My
baby would never have begun that night and then he wouldn't have
had to die before he was even born. I caused it all. I'm so sorry, so
very sorry for it all!"

"Jenny, none of this, none of it is your fault. You did nothing
wrong at all." He reached to tilt her face to his. "I don't know what
hellhole hatched the slime that harmed you and the baby, but I do
know it had nothing to do with you personally. Nothing you did
caused you to be raped and beaten. It happened. Just as it happens
every day even to tiny children and old women! You were a victim."

But he knew his words did not reach her. He could not dissuade her of her conviction that something in herself had drawn her
attacker. In turn, she felt the loss of the baby from her savaged body
a further judgment so that she bore a double burden, each more than
sufficient to break her courage.

She grew remote, so remote he was deeply uneasy. She spent long hours at the window, watching the river, her thoughts deep within. She no longer wept, but her eyes were haunted and full of her grief. She answered when he spoke to her but with a certain hesitation as if he called her back from some distant place.

Once he looked up from his desk to see her before the mirror by the bed. Her eyes were searching. She touched her breast and then her hands went up to savagely clutch and twist her hair, her face contorted by an expression of utter self-loathing. Her hands fell to cradle a life no longer there, and she turned away from the mirror, her spark of fury spent, and her desolation evident in the weary drop of her body.

He did not trust her, and he watched her through the days until at length she became aware he did. She seemed then to make an effort toward normalcy, but he was not deceived and kept his watch.

The day had been long after a sleepless night, and they were both tired. Also, that day Jenny had dressed in in own clothes and with her muffled into one of his jackets, he had taken her some distance down from the cabin, showing her the lay of the land and the sweep of the river through the valley.

The river seemed to draw her attention as it always drew his. From either bank, the ice crept out toward the center: brittle ice that could support no more than its own drape of snow. A little color had come into her face, and she seemed almost relaxed as if she had reached some decision and had found peace in it. Her eyes roamed the magnificent scenery: the mountains looming over them, their swath of snow punctuated by frosty firs and leafless trees, and the immensely blue sky far, far above them. Her eyes came back to the river and for a fleeting moment, he was surprised by a look of satisfaction on her face.

Back in the cabin, she seemed almost cheerful, sipping warmed wine after dinner while he put away their outdoor clothes and brought his glass to sit before the fire with her. Max stretched full length on the hearth between them, and the first of the evening light slanted into the room. St. Agnes rose in a few minutes and went out to shut a forgotten shed door. He came back with a streak of grease on his jeans and saw his hands were grimy as well. Tired anyway, he decided to shower, and they would make an early night of it. Jenny was still by the fire with her glass, her hand on Max's warm back, watching the fire; and after a moment, he left her there and went into the bath.

He never knew what warned him: what instinct working overtime saved them. He was standing barefoot in only his jeans about to start the water when suddenly he was fully alert. In the next moment, he was through the outside door running toward the river, following her flying figure down the steep slope. The last of the light gleamed rose amber on the dark water beyond the fine ice. She was quite some distance ahead, running like a swift shadow across the snow, her goal assured.

He shouted her name, just once, knowing the futility of calling out but unable to stop that one cry. She glanced back, stumbling a little, giving him a moment's gain, but he know he would never reach her before she made the water.

He became aware of Max racing toward her, too, in a long curving run that would reach her before he could. The dog was strong, the icy water his element. A chance lay with him, and he knew Max loved her, too.

Jenny reached the edge and was out across the fragile ice without hesitation. For a moment he thought it would hold her slight weight, but in the next, he saw the black water beneath the shattering ice, and saw her fall without a sound into the frigid water and out of sight.

Almost immediately, Max broke ice behind her, swimming strongly and diving after her moments before St. Agnes reached them. The shock of the water drove the breath from his lungs, and then he too gasped air and dove into the blackness. He could see nothing, nothing at all. But when Max surfaced, he had her firmly by her sweater, holding her head above the water, struggling toward the bank. The last of the light gleamed on their wet heads as they thrashed in the numbing cold: the dog and man fighting to bring the girl ashore; she struggling to evade their grasp. The whole scene was played out in silence save for their gasping breathes until the man called out her name in such despair she turned to look fully into his face. Her face held unendurable grief to match his despair.

"Jenny, dear God! Don't fight me!"

The cold was taking his strength, and he knew neither of them could last much longer. The water was too deep for him to stand and her clothing was pulling her down. His arms ached with the strain even though Max was supporting much of her weight. Their struggles had moved them closer to the swift current, and he felt it reaching greedily for them. He knew then unless she let him, they would die here in this wilderness for he would never leave her. The current caught him suddenly so that as she stared, the black water closed over his face and his grasp loosened.

She saw then that to fulfill her ambition was to take his life also and that she could not do. She longed in desperation for oblivion, and a rage rose in her that he would not let her drown, but as he surfaced, she put her hand to him and lent her own small strength to make the bank.

St. Agnes came up from the water with her in his arms. Thin sheets of ice formed and broke on his bare shoulders and chest as he somehow brought them up the hill to the cabin that floated like a lighted ship above them. Max shook himself dry and trotted beside them, wearied but not distressed. St. Agnes's breath came in ragged gasps, the exertion and cold taking their toll. Jenny's breath came as raggedly, and she shivered in great shakes, her body jerking convulsively.

Inside, he pulled her toward the bathroom, both of them stumbling and nearly falling. The bear lay by the door where she had dropped it, and she stopped short at seeing it. A moment and she was fighting him with all the strength of her rage and grief.

He let her rage, making no effort to subdue her, pulling her into the bathroom and stripping away her clothes. Holding her with one arm, he removed the last of his own clothing and took her with him into the hot shower. The water poured over them, driving out the awful cold. She leaned away against his supporting arm, hitting him over and over, pounding her fists on his chest and raking his shoulders with her nails until the blood flowed. Sobs choked her, and she cried out rage and pain while he held her without force under the streaming water and let her fight him.

At last as she tired, he caught her upraised hand in his, and said quietly, "Jenny, look at me." She saw the blood on his face and the compassion and the rage drained away so that she put her head down on his chest and let him draw her close. She clung to him, exhausted.

"Oh, Teddy, why didn't you let me go? Why won't you let me die? I want to so badly!"

CHAPTER 14

S he was in his arms all the night. She was sleeping when he came to the bed, and he could not bear to have her beyond his touch. He lay down with his hand on her wrist, but that grip shifted to take her into his arms, holding her tightly against him. Her breath came into his mouth as she slept, and he inhaled its perfume as an elixir for his terror. Sleep claimed them for long hours as their bodies recovered.

Jenny woke at last in the early noon to see St. Agnes with Max at the fire he had just built up. His hands deep in the dog's thick ruff, he brought their heads together as he praised him in a low caressing voice that overjoyed the animal. When St. Agnes arose and went into the kitchen, the dog followed him, knocking chairs about, and well content.

As the dog ate, St. Agnes stood watching the river, his face expressionless. Her footsteps were still visible in the snow. He turned at her slight movement and looked across the room at her without moving. He was unshaven and only half dressed, barefoot, his shirt not yet buttoned. In the clear morning light, she could see the marks of her nails on his chest and face. The sun struck against his shoulders and showed the set of his mouth as he at last came across the room to her. When he reached the bed, his manner eased and his expression gentled.

"Good morning, Jenny."

"Teddy—Christopher died."

He understood at once it was an explanation and an apology.

"Yes, I know. But you must live."

His voice was gentle but uncompromising. A muscle tightened in his jaw, and he reached out to smooth her hair from her cheek. He caught her hand in his.

"Promise me you'll never do this again, Jenny."

She looked at him with all her helpless grief in her too pale face.

"Teddy, why didn't you let me go? There's nothing for me to live for!"

He shook his head.

"Promise me, Jenny."

Again, she saw the marks on his face and body, knowing she had done that to him. His hand tightened on hers, and she felt again that frantic moment he had gone under the water and she had felt his iron grasp falter. He would have given his life!

"My life isn't worth that much, Teddy."

"Jenny…" For a moment, he hesitated. Then he said, "If your life means nothing to you, give it to me. It means all the world to me."

He spoke so quietly it seemed what he said was of no consequence but never thought to doubt him.

"Teddy—" She reached out to touch the long raking scratch at his throat and her eyes filled. "I have nothing left to give you. It's all been taken away. There's nothing left at all."

"Jenny, all I ask is your promise, nothing more. Let me be able to rest knowing you are safe, knowing you are mine."

"Teddy, I—"

"Are you still afraid of me, Jenny?"

"Oh, Teddy! I was never afraid of you, not you! Only of—of your being a man."

"I am a man, Jenny. That's part of me, too, but I promise I will never hurt you, never as long as I live."

His voice was comfort; all he had ever given had been care and comfort. She had nothing at all to give him in return save this one thing, so unimportant to her but seemingly of such value to him. How could she refuse him?

"I know in my heart you would never hurt me, Teddy, you never have. But I will probably be afraid again. I know I am of living. But I give you my promise to live and my life is yours."

She lay a moment, looking up into his face. He smiled, his mouth quite beautiful, and a curious feeling stirred in her.

"Teddy, why are you so good to me?"

His smile deepened to one of self-mockery. He reached out to lay his hand across her breast, the scar beneath his palm.

"I think my heart beats here," he said.

CHAPTER 15

꧁ꗞꗞꗞ꧂

Their days fell into a kind of order. St. Agnes worked on his articles and began the index for a medical text. Jenny was discouraged from disturbing the perceived confusion of his desk, but she proved an asset in organizing his random filing system. She worked quietly, a murmur of small activity that reassured him and left him free to work. As long as he knew she was near, he could turn his mind to the material.

When she thought him completely engrossed, she sat with a book in a nearby chair and watched him. He worked methodically for all the melee of notes and references. His surgeon's fingers flew over the keyboard. His face in profile was unfamiliar to her, so professional, strongly focused on his work with small lines between his brows and along his cheek. His absorption in his work frightened her in some way, as if he were far away from this warm room, gone beyond the thicket of firs on the hills that sheltered the cabin. She thought him totally absent in these hours at his desk; completely unaware of her or anything outside his scope of concentration.

She was wrong. St. Agnes knew where she was at any given moment.

He was also aware of how she watched him at his work. Like the little fox, she had placed almost complete trust in him. She no longer startled at a sudden move or took fright at his touch. Somehow, the fight for her life, their lives, followed by her outburst of rage and her attack on him, had proven a catharsis for her fear. In this atmosphere of trust, he hoped she would come to terms with her grief and guilt, opening the way for a relationship going far beyond simple trust and reliance. For quite simply, he meant ultimately to have her at his side always, a whole woman healed of her terror and remorse, finding the same joy he had in her presence.

Now he left her alone for long periods, giving her the space she needed to regroup and recover herself. He did not expect her to easily overcome her trauma, but he was aware their seclusion gave her limitless freedom to concentrate on her emotions without distraction. His manner was easy; he put no demands on her, asked no involvement. When she turned to him, he was there, his whole attention turned to her need with such depth she could not doubt his fidelity even as she sensed his withdrawal to the sidelines giving her an opportunity to regain her footing.

At first she spent long hours doing little more than watching the fire, her mind indeed turned inward touching her grief, knowing the need to fit it into her continuing life. To deny that grief was to deny her baby, something she could never do, and something she came to realize she was not meant to do. The baby would always be a part of her and in some strange way of St. Agnes, too, for in giving her the little bear, he acknowledged the child as if it were his own. Christopher would always be a part of them both, a sweetly remembered child whose unseen face would live in their memories. When this had been worked through, she took the baby bear, wrapped him lovingly in his blanket, and set him on a little bench near the bedroom.

Here her hand often touched him in passing, her fingers brushing over him softly, but never lingering too long.

When first she ventured outside, St. Agnes could not be at ease. He believed she would honor her promise but death had come too near, twice at her beckoning, and the last time had been on the boundary of no return. She was not the only one to have known real terror. He could hardly bear to look at his river now. But as she stood at the door, she turned to meet his eyes with her own steady look, and he said nothing, only giving her a small smile that cost him a great deal.

Max was still enough of a puppy to cajole her into play. St. Agnes was again thankful for the dog who wouldn't leave her alone to solitary exploration. Max tugged and pulled at her, worrying her walk until she ended in the snow with him. Triumphantly, he ran at her with little barks, inviting her chase. They romped like two children. Color came into her face as they played and her smile came more frequently. Her eyes were bright with the same exuberance as Max's. He had her hat and was running in small circles around her until he dropped it before her. She snatched it up, holding it over her head, and the dog leaped strongly for it, throwing her down, then standing over her growling with her hand clamped lightly in his jaws. St. Agnes' fingers stilled on the keyboard as he heard her laughter at last. She caught Max around his huge head, completely unimpressed with his pretended ferocity, and they resumed their tussle with equal pleasure. When at last they both tired, the dog lay with his head cocked to one side watching as she made a circle of snow angels as the day drew to a close.

She then spent most of the days outside while he worked. He asked her to stay within sight of the cabin and so she did. She soon found a favorite nook in an outcropping of rock where she could sit comfortably leaning back to watch the sky or looking down to the river. Her eyes roamed the mountains. Down the hillside, the river ran on cold and pure, intent only on its journey. She felt the continuity of life here. There was healing in the land.

She sat thus one morning until St. Agnes put aside his work and came to find her. She looked down to see him standing at the base of the rock and gave him such an uncomplicated smile; he blinked and felt a stab of joy.

He leaned back in his chair to watch her as she busied herself in the kitchen. Idly, he wondered if she would be able to cook if she couldn't catch her bottom lip between her teeth at crucial moments. She wore her usual indoor attire, one of his shirts or sweaters with rolled sleeves, barefoot and barelegged. Her mane of hair nearly reached her bottom. Now she reached up to a cabinet, and he smiled at her tsk of annoyance when she couldn't reach the handle. He switched off the computer and came to reach around her for the spice she wanted. He lifted a pot top, sniffing.

"What's this?"

She was a good cook, imaginative, with a style completely different from his own. The kitchen was invariably a disaster when she finished.

"Teddy," she said, ignoring his question, "will you take me walking sometime soon? I want to see everything, and I promised you to stay near."

"So you did, little one. And you've been true to your word. We'll go wherever you like this afternoon. You should have told me you wanted to go."

"I just have, Teddy," she said so reasonably he laughed.

They went for a distance to the back of the cabin where Jenny had not been before. It was quite cold, and Jenny was so bundled she could hardly walk. Their breath came in little clouds. Max trotted along with them; his eyes bright, his tail wagging with pleasure.

"Here is where Max found you," St. Agnes said in a rather strained voice. There was snow on her cheek and he reached to brush it away, wanting no reminder of a snow princess. She gave Max a hand to sniff and smiled.

As they passed the spot on their way back to the cabin, St. Agnes asked her if there were anything she needed from her snow-shrouded car. She shook her head no and in a moment added, "You don't bring a suitcase to a suicide."

The word lay starkly between them, but it had too much power to impress either of them. They both knew she had come to the mountain to die, had tried again, when the first attempt failed. Each knew well the insupportable grief that had brought her to seek death, and each knew equally well now she would never try again. He only smiled, as did she.

CHAPTER 16

Very gradually, he began to push her a little, to test the faith of his little fox, He went slowly, always giving her a chance for retreat, never bringing her even near the edge of fear. His lovemaking was very subtle but constant. As an old patient of his once expressed it, he "cut her no slack."

She, like the little fox, was hesitant but fascinated, ready to respond, ready to flee. He had promised to ask nothing of her, nor did he. The first sign of distress: a small frown, an uneasy gesture, and he gave it up with good grace. So easily did he withdraw, she often experienced a vague sense of loss and drew a little closer for his ready reassurance.

And he was her reassurance, always there to comfort her when the bad times came, did as they would perhaps for years. That he cared deeply she had no doubt; times he revealed more than he realized.

It had been an unconscious habit of his when he had let Max out for a last run before coming in for the night to stand watching the river running through the snow. Sometimes he delayed for long minutes to watch the moon on the river if the night were bright. The river had drawn him in the beginning to this particular place but now he could hardly stand the sight of it and turned his back as once he had turned his face. In time, Jenny saw this and understood.

One night he came to the window where she stood looking out, her face troubled in the faint light. She turned at his approach and put out a hand to him.

"Teddy," she said sadly, "look at your river. I can't bear it if I've taken that from you."

Against his will, he turned to look down as the swift black water wound like a mourning band on the white arm of snow; and his face hardened into remoteness. But her hand was on him still, urging him. In a few moments, he picked her up and sat down by the window where he could watch the rush of water. After a time, she fell asleep with her head on his shoulder, and the reality of her drowsing in his lap made possible his reconciliation with his river.

She had never seen him angry.

He worked all afternoon in the outbuildings, seeing to his truck and other equipment, including the backup generators that assured their power. It was all routine work kept routine by his regular attention. He had left a venison stew on a slow burner, an easythreating her as carefully as a child; meal as Jenny had seemed a little pale. Anxious as always, he had felt her pulse, never able to take her health casually. She had smiled and shook her head, saying only she was a little tired.

Now he came in, brushing snow from his wide shoulders, toughly masculine in his heavy outdoor clothing, to find her in pain. She lay on her side with her knees drawn up, her arms crossed over her abdomen, her white face buried in the pillow.

"Jenny!" He came to the bed, deeply frightened, and then understanding, deeply angry. "How long have you been like this?"

He threw off his heavy jacket, the fur still dripping melted snow and went for his medical bag as he spoke.

Her voice, faint and careful, came in shallow breaths from the top of her lungs, told him how much pain she was suffering.

"Just a while—" She stopped when saw the syringe in his hand and shut her eyes against the sting. It came quickly, so lightly she barely felt his touch. In minutes, he saw her begin to relax; and he wiped the perspiration from her brow, thankfully seeing the tension leave her face. He drew the coverlet over her shoulders, easing her into comfort. The gentleness of hands belied the harshness of his face.

"Is it always like this?" he asked, knowing the answer.

"No," she said distantly, beginning to drowse. "This is the first time. Dr. Hergert said it might be this way. It may get better after a few months, he said."

He arose, unable to sit still for his rage. He made a turn about the room seeing her huddled figure, so small in her undeserved pain. He cursed savagely.

She opened her eyes in amazement, seeing his fury for the first time. His face was white and a muscle jerked in his jaw. He prowled the room, his fists clenched in impotent anger. Far from being frightened, she found a kind of comfort in his anger and lay nestled. Soon she slept.

And in the night when the heavy cramps returned, beginning to arouse her, she felt again the quick sting of the needle and slept again. He sat by the bed, his hand bent to the small hand he held.

He would never have thought to call these incidents lovemaking.

CHAPTER 17

⟨∭⟩

She sat at the fire, her bare legs gleaming in the firelight. An open book of Audubon bird prints lay on the hearth before her, and as she leaned over it, her hair swung in her way. She pushed it back repeatedly, until she became conscious of the irritation. She put both hands up, lifting the mane of curls, and looked around for something to secure them. Behind her on the couch, St. Agnes glanced up from the work draft on his knee and in turn looked vaguely about the room for some restraint. She smiled and shook her head, one arm crossed over her head, the curls springing between her fingers. She leaned back to her book, still holding her hair, so the firelight now revealed the pure lines of her face and throat. He was watching her now, his work forgotten.

"Teddy, look here. I've seen this one, haven't you?"

He leaned over her shoulder to look, his face near hers. One of the little curls by her temple escaped to tickle his mouth and he blew it to one side, his breath warm on her cheek.

"Yes, that one, and"—he turned a page—"this one, too. They're common here. This one you'll see a lot of in the spring."

In a few minutes, she closed the book, frowning a little so that he waited.

"Teddy, in the spring…We'll have to go back, won't we?"

She could not know what reassurance it was to him to hear her say "we."

"Yes, I'm afraid we will—sometime in the spring. I've no commitments until late in the season, but there'll be things to be done."

She did not question "things to be done." They had discussed this before. But her frown deepened, her troubled thoughts running on.

"Teddy, I never was very good at meeting people and now I—it's hard to…to trust—."

She got up in agitation, turning to face him, the light outlining her body but now shadowing her face. He set his work completely aside, looking up at her, the same light revealing his face clearly.

"You can relearn trust, Jenny," he said lightly. "Take it one person at a time. Start with me." His voice was deceptively lazy, his eyes the same. He held out his hand. "I'll never hurt you. Come to me."

There was something in his gaze that kept her where she was.

"I do trust you, Teddy," she said somewhat uncertainly. "I know you won't hurt me. You never have."

"That's knowledge, sweetheart, not trust. Come."

There was still something in his face and voice, intriguing, not quite frightening but she held her place.

"I think not."

He laughed then, letting her off, and held out his hand again. She came then, settling into his arms, his cheek to hers as they faced the fire.

"Don't worry, Jenny. I'll always be there. It'll be all right." His quiet confidence in her was as steady as his heartbeat.

After a time, she stirred.

"Teddy, don't most men want to marry a virgin?"

This convention had been bound to come.

"I suppose most men would say so. It's fairly typical for a man to ask one thing, to be another."

She considered this and a faint blush showed on the cheek nearest his. She drew breath, hesitated, and then said nothing.

"I didn't know you were coming along, Jenny," he said quietly. She glanced quickly at him without turning, and after a moment, a small smile moved her mouth, and she laid her head against his shoulder.

"But doesn't it bother you, Teddy?"

"What?" he asked deliberately.

"Not to marry a virgin?"

"What do you fancy I have on my lap?" he asked comfortably, his eyes on the impossibly high arch of her bare foot."

She was shocked.

"Teddy, you can't mean that! You know—" Her voice changed, holding the note of shame he despised and as abruptly, his mood changed. He swung her around to face him.

"I know what?" he demanded. "I know you were attacked and beaten almost to death. That is what I know and will always know how close I came to losing you without ever knowing you. But that is all I know! Had he beaten you and nothing more, would you question me? If it is so important to you, as it is not to me, you are as virgin as a lily! You have known no man! Please God someday I will be the first, the last, the only! By His Grace, someday I hope to bring you to such a passion as to burn every thought of that night from your mind forever. But know this, Jenny, if I had found you in a brothel, you would still be what I want, all I will ever want!"

She was staring at him, her eyes wide. He cursed himself for saying far more than he had ever thought to say, far more than he thought she was ready to hear, and he feared her withdrawal. But she said nothing, nor did she move from his arms. Rather, she reached out and touched his mouth with her fingers, tracing the line of his lips, and then buried her face in his throat, holding close against him.

He never referred to that night's conversation, nor did she; but watching her as always, he thought she moved with more assurance and he thanked God.

CHAPTER 18

They sat at breakfast New Year's Day. The smell of fresh baked bread filled the room as the sun poured into the room, glancing rainbows through the icicles outside the window and shimmering on the table. Max as always was carefully licking the marmalade off his toast before eating it. Jenny glanced at St. Agnes as she reached for the orange juice, seeing the sun in his very blond hair and on the backs of his wrists. He wore a blue sweater the color of his eyes. He looked up, caught her watching him and smiled, the crease leaping to his cheek. Jenny felt a little catch about her heart.

"Did you make any New Year's resolutions, Teddy?" she asked rather at random.

He was still smiling.

"A few," he said. "And did you?"

"Well, no, not yet. I'm still thinking about it."

He stood up to bring them more coffee.

"My mother used to have to suggest mine for me. I could never think of much more than resolving to learn karate to beat up George Hicks."

"Who was George Hicks?" she asked, looking up as he set her cup down.

"The school bully. He used to beat me up regularly when I was in second grade. I think he was in first."

She looked across her cup at him. He looked very capable, tough.

"That's hard to imagine now. Did you ever learn karate?"

"Not in time to help with George. He moved away at the end of the school year. I've always regretted it."

She laughed.

"What did your mother suggest for your resolutions?"

"Oh, things to better my soul, to make me the 'right kind of man,' things like that, and keeping my room clean and doing my homework. Nothing that seemed worth spending a lot of time on." His love for his mother was very evident in his voice.

"Well, I don't know about your room, but you must have done your homework. And you certainly succeeded in the rest."

"Why, Jenny," he said lightly, "you do care."

"Teddy, don't tease!"

"Why ever not?" he questioned, his eyes very bright. "Would you like me to suggest a resolution for you? Come! Let me hold you so I can think better. No? Then at least give me your hand."

He reached across the table and took her hand into his, turning her palm up and tracing the lines with his finger.

"Well, I can see you are a young woman of great beauty, but then I already knew that, didn't I? Your charm line is very long, too. Ah, here we are, the lines of love and passion, very long but very faint. I think you should resolve to strengthen those lines, preferably, in fact definitely, with me in mind. I'd be delighted to help you."

He gave her back her hand, still smiling. She was saved from answering by Max's demand for more jelly.

The middle of January brought a huge snow and ice storm. Jenny sat in the window seat between fire and ice, stitching contentedly on a needlework project that had belonged to St. Agnes's mother. It was a big undertaking barely begun. And had been stored away with all its needles and thread intact. Jenny wouldn't take out the little his mother had done but neatened the stitches and wove them in with quick practiced skill. St. Agnes, looking over her shoulder, laughed.

"Mom was never very good at that sort of thing, but she always had hope. She left that the last summer she was here. I was to hang it over the bed. I made the frame as an act of faith. I think she would be glad you're doing it for her."

As Jenny stitched, she thought about his mother and the resolutions she had made for her son. She must have been proud of the
man he had become. If Christopher had lived, she would have hoped
to rear him to be as fine a man. His name came easily into her mind
now. She glanced at the little bear and smiled.

Resting her eyes, she looked across the room through the arch to
the study where he was working. He was frowning over some paper,
a pen held ready for corrections. His hand on the pen looked sure,
strong. She thought of his hand on her arm, pulling her with him
into the shower. He had let her rage against him, endured her abuse,
and then drawn her close.

That had gone a long way toward her healing, but she knew
she was not yet completely well. She no longer feared St. Agnes but
he treated her like a cherished child, nothing more. She had made
a promise of her life to him, and she would honor that promise;
indeed, she couldn't conceive of a life without him. But what sort
of bargain had he made for himself? When he turned to her as hus-
band to wife, lover to lover, would she be able to respond? She was
inexperienced in the ways of a man with a woman. Desire had never
been more than vague girlish stirrings linked with visions of moonlit
gardens and wedding dresses.

In spite of her real beauty, she had never attracted more than the
passing attention of the young men she had worked around; the easy
sexual banter and suggestive talk of her coworkers had passed over
her without understanding. Now she knew herself not to be normal
without knowing what was normal.

There was no one she could turn to, no one to advise her. She
wished desperately she could have known his mother. Somehow,
she felt she would have been a person Jenny could turn to, a warm
woman who would have welcomed the broken girl her son had cho-
sen. Now there was no one to ask save St. Agnes himself, and her
growing awareness of him made the subject impossible to broach.
She knew she could trust him without limit, and her faith in him
was absolute, but she didn't know how to react to her attraction to
him. His touch, his manner drew her, but when she felt the need to

withdraw, she had no way of judging her retreat as natural as a result of the attack.

She sighed without being aware she did. St. Agnes looked up to see her troubled face and wondered where her thoughts had taken her. It was difficult for him to maintain his careful attitude. He loved her deeply and fiercely and wanted nothing more than to hold her and show her his love. He was at the same time very aware of her inexperience and of the aftereffects of rape. There would be times in loving her, in arousal, when he could inadvertently frighten her or bring back the rape. For this very reason, he knew the path to physical intimacy must be taken slowly. She must trust him every step of the way. Knowing this and angrily compassionate, he was impatient with himself for the pressing physical hunger that grew naturally with his love.

Now he put aside his papers, stood up, stretched, and went down to the basement for an armload of wood. When he came up, Jenny had folded away the needlework and was in the kitchen beginning their meal. She seemed preoccupied, and he left her to the task, although they usually worked together. He felt a bit on edge tonight himself.

He went downstairs again, started a load of laundry, swept the floor around the wood stack, and then still restless, busied himself straightening the canned goods on the pantry shelves. The aroma of the meal drifted down and he could hear Jenny talking to Max as she worked. He took a load of clothes from the drier and started the ones he had washed. He folded the clothes, all of them his, but certain ones thought of now as Jenny's. Her own clothes were held in reserve for their trips outside. She had taken to sleeping in an ancient sweatshirt of his, which so far as he was concerned was a much better choice than the top of a pair of satin pajamas his sister Alecia had given him in what he thought of as a fit of madness.

Jenny called down the stairs to him, and he brought the folded laundry with him as he came. After dinner, he cleared away and did the dishes while the wind continued outside, occasionally rattling a window and making the house warm and secure. Jenny brought up the other clothes from the drier and put them away, coming into the kitchen to put dish towels in the drawer next to the sink where he stood. It was growing dark outside, and he could see their reflections in the window glass. Jenny's hair, unkempt, was a mass of long silky curls that seemed to have a life of their own, and the sweater she wore was an especially large one so that it kept sliding down from one shoulder. It came almost to her knees and was, as he knew, all she had on. Now as she leaned past him, the sweater slipped again revealing for a moment the little scar.

"Jenny?"

"Yes, Teddy?" She looked up quickly wondering if she had displeased him in some way. He had been distant all evening, hardly talking at all during dinner.

The expression on her face gave him pause. Whatever he had been about to say left him. He reached out and let one of the curls wrap itself around his finger.

"Whatever is troubling you, Jenny," he said, "let it go."

She shook her head and the ringlet slipped away with the swirl of hair that hid her face as she closed the drawer and turned away.

"There's nothing, Teddy."

He caught her arms as she made to walk past him, his hold very light, careful as always not to seem overpowering. She couldn't hide the sudden color in her face, and he was intrigued. Before she realized his intention, he swung her up and set her by the sink.

"Now then, what is it, baby?"

"Teddy. Put me down!"

"No." He smiled. "Let's talk a bit. Tell me what you've been thinking of all afternoon. I truly, truly would love to know."

"No," she said, but she saw no way of getting down modestly without his help. She looked back into his face and what she saw brought the color flooding into her own.

"Teddy, please put me down!"

"In a minute, sweetheart. Were you thinking of me?" Her lashes swept down at that and he laughed. "So you were!"

She said quickly, her color still high, "I was thinking of your mother, Teddy, and how much I wish I could have known her."

"Yes, I wish you could have known each other. She would have loved you. You two could have talked about me," he added with another laugh.

"That's what I mean!" she said involuntarily.

"Really? What about me, Jenny?"

She looked away, past him, her bottom lip caught in small white teeth. He waited, watching the expressions chase across her face.

"Oh, just things," she said vaguely, shaking her head. She touched her top lip with her tongue, a provocation he knew to be innocent but nevertheless quite potent. He touched her mouth softly with his thumb.

"Can't you tell me about them?"

"No! I couldn't tell mean, just if I—if you—How—!"

"You sound muddled, little one."

He was still looking at her mouth, and now he seemed to come to some decision. He looked up to meet her eyes directly.

"Now's the time to scream if you're going to, sweetheart. I must warn you, I'm going to kiss you."

Her eyes widened as his hand moved to slip beneath her chin, lifting her face to his. For just a moment, he hesitated, and then he bent to her mouth. He was very gentle, his lips at first only brushing hers, leaving to touch her cheek fleetingly, then coming back to claim her mouth as his own for long, long moments of deep sweetness. He felt her tremble deeply and lifted his head, feeling her shaken breath on his cheek, but she didn't move, and he lowered his mouth to hers again.

A long time later, he asked against her lips, "Are you afraid of me again, Jenny?" for she was shaking so she held to his shirt with both hands. Her whispered no was very faint, but he heard her and took it as permission to kiss her again.

Max's impatient woof at last recalled them. St. Agnes looked down at the girl in his hands, reluctant to let her go. Her face was warmly flushed, and there was a languid look about her brilliant eyes. He lifted her down; she looked up and, the flush deepened when she saw he meant to kiss her again.

When he lifted his head this time, he was smiling.

"I can't remember just what we were talking about, but I know I've never enjoyed a conversation more, Jenny! We should have these talks more often!"

He was whistling as he finished cleaning the kitchen.

CHAPTER 19

A nd so they continued. At times, his desire became so insistent he quit the cabin and invented work in the outbuilding or, inwardly grimacing at the cliché, split great stacks of firewood. Anything that took him from her and exhausted him was welcomed. He was so overwhelmingly conscious and as completely unable to shut her from his thoughts.

When she was in his arms, he schooled himself to casualness, treating her as carefully as a child; all the while longing to bury his face in her throat, to caress her, to kiss her never into submission but into a passion to meet his own. He had not kissed her since the evening in the kitchen, and it took all he had within him to refrain, to slow the tempo, to continue only an easy steady courtship, biding his time, giving her time.

And Jenny sought to deal with her own growing response. She knew St. Agnes loved her, and one morning she woke before him. And lying beside him, listening to his steady breathing, and watching the morning sun touch his features, she realized she loved him, too: deeply and absolutely, and for his own sake, not for his loving her.

She lay quietly with her face pillowed on her hands. She saw the power and strength and sensuality of his face and body and was completely unafraid of his maleness. The light ran across his morning beard and the hair on his arms and chest, and she longed to follow the roaming sun with her fingers, to kiss him awake, to tell him of her great discovery. Almost she put out her hand, only to check at once as St. Agnes stirred.

He came awake in time to catch her unguarded expression before she could turn away. He lay very still without moving, watching the color rise in her face. He smiled at her confusion, making no effort to hide the desire in his eyes.

"What a lovely sight to begin the day," he said softly. He reached out and took her hand, drawing her to him. "Do you have a kiss for me, Jenny?"

Her color deepened, darkening, and widening her eyes. She sat up quickly, still turned toward him as if drawn by some force. The satin shirt she was wearing again revealed the tightness of her breasts, and her hair floated in sunshine around her rapt face. Her hand was still in his so that he sat up with her, powerful, faintly aggressive, so that her breath caught. She swayed toward him as though her body had a will of its own. With a strength he didn't know he had, he resisted the urge to take her into his arms. Instead still holding her hand, he put his other hand in her curls and brought her mouth slowly to his. She leaned into his kiss, her mouth moving faintly beneath his so that he felt the fire throughout his body.

At last he released her, as much at a loss for words as she seemed to be. He looked down at their hands, still clasped, to find her fingers wound tightly around his thumb. At this unconscious gesture, symbolic of her reliance on him, on his care, he recalled himself and swung from the bed, leaving her staring after him.

St. Agnes sat by the fire cleaning his rifle as Jenny finished the dishes. He had seen the tracks of a moose too near the cabin, and there was always the possibility of a rogue. He had noted too the nearness of the wolf pack and thought the moose might be their objective. Although he was not really concerned with the wolves' presence, he had seen Max's interest. The dog was half wolf himself and seemed to feel the call of his wild relatives.

Jenny came to join him sitting on the rug at his feet. She watched him for a while, handing him things as he needed them, and then she got up and fetched her needlework. They busied themselves in silence, content at the moment in their nearness.

"Teddy. Tell me about your father. Do you remember him at all?" She knew his father had died in a boating accident when St. Agnes was very young.

He glanced up from the rifle and smiled.

"Yes, I remember him very well. I was seven and Alecia was four. I don't think she remembers him much at all, but I have very good memories of him."

He ran the polishing cloth along the stock.

"He was built like a football player, and he was one in college. He was full of laughter and fun. He spent a lot of time with his family, his children, and my mother adored him. I remember they were together and he worshipped her in return. Even at seven, I think I knew what a special thing they had together. Then he was killed. For a long time, the laughter was all gone, and then slowly it came back as though he sent it back to her. She never remarried. She never felt herself a widow. He was just somewhere else for a while."

"Teddy, how wonderful. How you must miss them both!"

"Yes, I do. But now they have each other again. I can't begrudge them that."

He smiled at her again. "I wish you had had a happier time of it."

He knew she had been orphaned quite early and had spent her childhood between two elderly and reluctant great aunts. There had been only enough money to send her to a community college, and she had been on her own for nearly three years.

She had had no one at all to fall back upon when she was in need. He reached out and touched her cheek, careful of the oil on his hand, and she smiled and shook her head.

"It doesn't matter. I managed."

His answering smile was rather tight.

"You'll never have to 'manage' again, Jenny. We'll be together the rest of the way, and we'll do far more than manage, I promise you!"

He snapped the rifle back together and stood to replace it in the gun case. He turned then to gather up his supplies and went to wash his hands, touching her hair as he passed. She worked on, content with her thoughts.

Other evenings and other times were not spent as peacefully.

Jenny sat cross-legged before the fire, her favorite spot, playing solitaire and listening to music. Max was with her, his interested nose at the edge of her cards, and she was playing as much with the dog as with any idea of a game. St. Agnes at his desk found he was unable to concentrate for her frequent low laughter and finally gave himself up to watching her. Each time she put down a card, the dog would half rise to sniff at it, invariably shifting the card with his breath, so that she must reposition each play. St. Agnes would have almost sworn the dog was laughing, too.

After a time, they tired of the game. Max went to sleep on the rug, and Jenny came to put the cards away, which for some reason were kept in St. Agnes's desk. He looked up, aware she was wearing what he considered that damnable pajama top. For some reason, he was feeling intensely irritated. She met his look and an expression he, if asked, would have called sulky crossed her face, taking up residence about her mouth.

She said nothing, nor did he, only opening the drawer for her to replace the cards.

She turned and walked away. He watched her cross the room to sit down in the window seat with her knees drawn up, the full moon's cold light on her averted face. He turned back to his neglected work with a sharp smothered sigh and managed to complete several paragraphs before he looked at her again.

When he did look, he saw she was worrying the little star scar with angry fingers.

She dropped her hand and turned again to the river, her face closed and remote. A moment and her hand came to her breast again with the same scorn, as if cruelly mocking an imperfection. Her mouth still looked sulky, and he thought she was near tears. Had she been a three year old, he would have thought she needed spanking and kissing.

He shut off the screen and stood up with an audible snap that brought her angry eyes to his. He walked to her without speaking or taking his eyes from hers and raised her from the window cushion. Still holding her eyes with his own, he quite deliberately unbuttoned the pajama shirt almost to her waist. He pushed it back from her shoulder, exposing her perfect uplifted breast. He looked then from her face to her breast and with the same deliberation, his hands encircled her. Holding her captive but with his hands light on the bunched satin around her waist, he bent his head and kissed the little scar. He felt the swift intake of her breath that drew her taut nipple across his cheek, but he only touched his mouth again to the scar before he stood. He pulled the shirt back across her breasts and put her carefully from him. He turned, caught up his parka in passing, and went out into the night, shrugging into the jacket.

He was still in the generator room when she went to bed, and when he came to bed, she was asleep. He could see the trace of tears on her cheek. He lay down and in a moment, reached out and drew her sleeping form into his arms. He slept finally; her back spooned to him and his face in her hair.

CHAPTER 20

In the morning, St. Agnes took Max with him a distance up the river and then turned to climb the slope behind the cabin. He saw more evidence of the wolves and coming back along the ridge, he found the print of a single moose. Again, it was nearer than he felt safe. He would have to warn Jenny to keep inside unless he were with her until he could be sure there was no danger. Imagining the reaction this was sure to bring, he laughed, making Max bark. The tension of the evening before was gone from his bearing; and an expression of great tenderness and something more, something that would have brought her quick color swept across his face. He laughed again and turned downhill, circling around to come along the river back up to the cabin.

He came in, stood his rifle by the door, and took off his heavy clothing. Jenny was standing in a chair tiptoeing up to search a cabinet. She had been rather subdued at breakfast, but now intent on her task, she turned to him naturally.

"Teddy, do you know where the nutcracker is? I've hunted everywhere!"

He came across to steady her as he reached into the drawer at her bare feet and took out not one but two nutcrackers. She looked at them with disgust and moved to come down. As she did, the chair beneath her tilted and only his arm about her waist saved her a fall. He lifted her free of danger and set her down, kissing the nape of her neck as he did.

"Oh, you're cold!"

"Do you really think so? Come warm me then, desire of my heart."

He laughed at her retreat to the fireplace. He made no move to follow her, however, giving her the courage to ask foolishly.

"Do you desire me, Teddy?"

"What a question to ask so early on a winter's morn!"

He stared at her until she began to blush. Little curls tipped with sunshine sprang along the length of her hair. Her skin showed no imperfection anywhere but glowed as if the light fell on satin. The lines of her slender body were totally familiar to him, at the same time, totally unknown, an exquisite torment he found at times quite maddening.

As he continued to stare at her, she touched her lips with her tongue in a little nervous gesture, and at that, his face changed. The laughter was gone and something very male took its place. Her breath caught, and she took a step backward although he hadn't moved. He smiled without amusement.

"What did you say? Do I what? Do I desire you?"

His voice was suddenly quite low and quite furious.

"Desire you?" he said again. "Well, let's define desire so we're talking from the same page. If you mean am I aware of every move you make, every tone and nuance of your voice, of how you look and feel and move, and how your beautiful hair slides across your shoulders and how your lashes sweep down when you look away, and the way your skin takes the light, and the fragile look of your wrists, shall I go on? Then yes, I would say I desire you! I'd love to take you in my arms and hold you like a kitten and run my hands down your straight little back, put my mouth in that hair, feel your heartbeat against mine while I track down the sweet elusive scent of your body. Yes, I really would! And you stand there across the room and call me Teddy, a ridiculous name only my mother ever called me, and ask if I desire you!"

He reached for his discarded jacket.

"But don't worry, flower face! I'm not going to do one damned thing about it. You're as safe with me as if you were a child until you come to me yourself! God grant the day!"

The door for once slammed behind him as he crossed the porch, shrugging into his parka.

After that, he refused to touch her at all. He warned her from the outdoors, turning a deaf ear to her outraged protests, and then spent as much time as possible outside himself. When the short winter days ended, he busied himself at his desk, finishing and setting aside the series of seminar lectures and the papers to be presented at the upcoming medical conferences. When he had finished those, he turned to the work, he had begun on a textbook and forced himself to hold his attention there without interruption.

He spoke pleasantly, if briefly, on things of no consequence and never allowed the conversation to even border on the personal. He never approached the bed unless he was absolutely certain she was thoroughly asleep and then he slept as far away as possible, denying them both the sweetness and comfort of her in his arms. Neither slept very well. He refused to let himself see the bereft look in her eyes or the slight drop in her posture.

He came in to lunch one noon and saw at once she had been crying. He made no reference to her streaked face but ate quickly and went out again. In his workshop then, he prowled around, frustrated and aching for them both. He finally slammed down a wood rasp so hard he broke the piece of wood he had been shaping for a frame, wasting several hours work.

Even Max seemed out of sorts. He disappeared for long hours at a time, and St. Agnes was sure the dog was tracking the pack for whatever reasons of his own. He didn't want to chance losing Max, and he was concerned the persistent moose could be a danger to the dog also, but he would not pen the animal. Now he knelt in the snow, worrying the dog's big head in his hands, his voice caressing him, but Max was only half-listening, turning away from his knee to look toward the woods. At last, St. Agnes released the dog and watched him run up the slope and disappear above the cabin.

And from the kitchen, Jenny watched St. Agnes, wondering how she could have been so foolish as to have provoked him. She knew he did desire her deeply. Her awareness of her own desire told her how much and with that same awareness, she could measure the curb he held on himself. She missed his lovemaking until she felt she could not endure another moment if he did not turn to her.

But turn he did not. He continued without break in the pattern he had set for their lives: a pattern he had ordained she must be the one to change. This she could not bring herself to do. Her love was so great it left her shaken. She wanted with all her heart to show him that love, but she was afraid.

Not of him! There was nothing he could do that would bring her to fear.

Her love and trust were too great. There was much, a very great much, of sexual lovemaking she had little or no idea of, but she knew her lover and her faith in him was without boundaries.

But she was afraid of herself. She had failed in so much! She couldn't bring him virginity, and it was unthinkable to her not to come as a virgin to his bed. She knew he regretted and raged at that loss only for the circumstances that had taken it without his being there to protect her, but she could not yet dissuade herself of the thought some hidden aspect of her character had caused her rape. It seemed incredible one human being could so attack another without reason.

That she had not been able to carry her baby to term seemed yet another judgment of failure. There too was the possibility there could never be another child, and surely, St. Agnes would want his son. Men did, she was sure. How could she face him if there were no child?

Even the painful monthly cycles seemed to sneer "damaged goods." She had never had more than the mildest of discomfort before, and now there was no certainty her periods would ever become easier. St. Agnes watched the calendar with her same apprehension.

If bedded, how could she be sure she would be what he would expect from his wife? Perhaps there would be such pain the very act would prove impossible. Perhaps the horror of that night would intervene making her unable to respond to him. Her own hunger left her trembling at the thought of his hands, his mouth, and his love-making, but would she be able to express herself? Perhaps even if all else were overcome, she herself would prove a disappointment, and he would find himself betrayed into an inadequate intimacy.

All these thoughts stayed her from reaching toward him. And he, guessing much of what went on in her mind, willed himself quiet to let her work it out for herself. He had shown her his love over and over again; she could not doubt him, and now she must learn not to doubt herself. This she must do on her own. He would be forever there to receive her, but she must make a leap of faith. He saw her struggle and her tears, but he made no move to help her.

CHAPTER 21

A fortnight passed, and Max continued his restlessness. He came in on an afternoon but disappeared the next morning. Jenny was anxious when the evening came and the dog did not, and St. Agnes was more concerned than he would admit. He went out on the porch several times and stood for long moments. She knew he was not watching his river but looking in the direction Max had taken. They were both relieved when at last very late Max's scratch at the door marked his return. He suffered their welcome and went to sleep by the fire almost immediately.

Jenny went to bed soon after that, leaving St. Agnes settled now at his desk, deep in his notes. She was not to know that when her regular breathing told him she slept, he drew his chair beside the bed and sat for a long time just looking at her.

She slept restlessly, and as she turned in her sleep, her hands came up in small fists to scrub at the smudged circles beneath her eyes. The light over his shoulder fell on her soft mouth with its little droop and his heart smote him for her grief. Her hands fell away to lie by her head as innocently as a child's. In the enveloping folds of his shirt, she looked little more than a child, a lovely girl child on the cusp of womanhood. Still child or not, she was his wife, his Eve, fashioned and given him by the Holy God Himself. She turned again, and he was as astonished as always by her beauty. He sighed and went to settle the house for the night.

At breakfast, he looked ruefully at the shadows under her eyes, wondering how long this would go on. He sighed inwardly, and went out with Max, resigned to waiting for both of them, woman and dog, to make their choices. Max disappeared at once into the woods, and St. Agnes, armed with binoculars and rifle, turned to climb the slope behind the cabin, looking for some sign of the wolves and the moose he was sure they were tracking.

Without even Max's company, Jenny's day was long. The cabin was too quiet, and music and the crackle of the fire only added to the stillness. She worked on the almost completed needlework and read a little until midafternoon. St. Agnes did not come in for lunch as he had said he would not, and Jenny realized she was hungry. She decided to slice some of the sourdough bread she had made earlier for a sandwich. She kept glancing out the window as she had all day, watching for St. Agnes and paying little attention to the job at hand. Suddenly she heard the distant but sharp crack of the rifle, twice. She startled so the knife slipped in a smooth, momentarily painless slice across her finger.

The sight of her blood didn't dismay her, but she was getting it everywhere. She held her finger under the faucet but the blood kept streaming with the water, so finally she wrapped her finger in a dishcloth, swiped at the blood on the countertop, and went to hunt a bandage.

There were none in the bathroom and none in his medical bag so she went down to the basement to look in the pantry where she found gauze. Since she was in the basement anyway, she started the washer, filling to soak the dishcloths and over the sound of the water didn't hear St. Agnes when he entered the cabin.

He looked about for her as he put the gun back in the cabinet, thinking he probably should have shot the moose instead of trying to scare it further into mountains away from the wolves that were certainly after it. He saw the blood on the dishcloth and in the sink just as Jenny saw the spider behind her in the basement.

Even the slaps from her exasperated aunts had never been able to stop Jenny's immediate and violent reaction to spiders. She screamed involuntarily and turned deathly white; her hands became clammy and a wave of nausea left her faint. St. Agnes reached the stairs and was down them just as the unfortunate spider scuttled toward her, and she screamed again.

"Jenny! For God's sake! What is it? Where have you hurt yourself? Jenny!"

He shook her a little. She was trembling, unable to answer, pointing to the floor with her free hand. The other was pressed to her mouth, trying to hold back another scream. He turned, letting go of her when he saw where she pointed. He killed the luckless spider and dropped it in the dustbin. She was still trembling when he turned back to her, but he didn't touch her save to take her clumsily bandaged hand. She was still too upset to notice what he was doing as he unwound the gauze and but when he pressed around the wound, she attempted to snatch her hand away.

"That hurts, Teddy!"

"Did you put antiseptic on this?"

He knew she had not and was already turning her toward the stairs.

"It's just a little cut. And it doesn't need anything. It washed clean. It bled a lot."

"That I know," he said tightly. The kitchen had seemed full of blood. "But you still need something on it. Go to the bathroom."

He sent her up the steps ahead of him as he turned back to bring the roll of bandages. She waited in the bathroom looking at him like a child about to be punished. He laughed shortly as he set the gauze down and took an antiseptic from the medicine cabinet.

"Jenny, it won't hurt. Give me your hand now."

He poured the antibiotic with a liberal hand until he was satisfied there would be no infection.

"There! Be brave now while I bandage it."

"I am brave, Teddy," she said somewhat suspiciously as she was still trembling, but he looked up at that, his eyes sweeping her face.

"I know you are, sweetheart," he said quietly.

Her eyes flew to his face and her mouth did tremble. Her hand turned in his as he finished the bandage. He was so close, but so forbidding.

"Oh, Teddy, please! Please hold me for just a moment," her voice fell to a whisper as she begged him. "Please, Teddy!"

For a breathless moment, she thought he would relent. Then he shook his head, denying her.

"No, Jenny, I don't think I would be able to let you go if I did."

He allowed her hand a moment longer and then withdrew. She was too proud to cling, but she thought her heart would stop.

"Teddy...do you still love me?" The question was wrong from her.

He looked at her gravely. The line of his mouth was so sweet it took her breath.

"My darling, you're too intelligent for that one. You know I love you. Now, forever, always. Be sure of that!"

Her throat moved.

"Teddy, I love you so!"

His mouth twisted but he said nothing, only looking at her. She looked away and then back to him.

"Teddy, I'm...I'm—" She closed her eyes against the sight of him and found the courage to continue. "You—you've had other women. Won't you please just take me?"

"Why in the world would I do that, Jenny?" He sounded astonished. She tried again.

"Teddy, I don't know if—if I can—and then I'd know now before—"

He stared at her coldly.

"I'm damned if I'll be part of any experiment! Either you love me and trust me or you do not! I've never 'taken' a woman nor will I begin now! Certainly, there have been other women. I am a good deal older than you, and I never dreamed there would be a you. They were never more than casual ties. You have no need to think otherwise."

He frowned, his look still one of hauteur. "I don't like talking of this to you, but there it is. They knew what we were about. I regret there was even one. 'Take' you! God forbid! When you're ready for what we will share, you'll have to come to me!"

She made as if to speak but he interrupted her, unable to hear it.

"Don't look to catalogue your supposed shortcomings to me, Jenny. I can see none!" His face was grim and his mouth set, but his eyes moved over her like a caress.

Her love with the sadness and ache were all in her voice.

"Teddy, I want you so!"

"Then come to me, Jenny!"

But he didn't wait for her response. He moved her from the door and went out, leaving her alone.

CHAPTER 22

By the time Max came in the next morning, St. Agnes had had enough.

He would pen the dog until the wolf pack moved out of the area or Max lost interest in following them. Jenny was wearing herself out and couldn't support the added worry over the dog.

Jenny saw the moose above the cabin, its huge shape blurred by the flurrying snow. There had not been fresh snow for some time, and she was sitting in the window seat, watching the flakes dance down. For the longest time, the moose simply stood there, brooding over the valley. Then at last, it turned and disappeared before she thought to draw St. Agnes' attention. When she looked his way, he appeared deep in frowning concentration at his desk, and she glanced away without speaking.

The snow continued all afternoon, and Max showed no interest in going out. St. Agnes worked on, and Jenny invented small tasks until she could find no more and took a nap in a chair by the fire. As always, when she slept, St. Agnes could not keep his eyes from her.

They had an early supper as the night closed in. St. Agnes took Max out for a run and again the dog seemed satisfied to be in by the fire. Jenny took her bath and washed her hair then sat with Max while she dried what seemed yards of soft dark curls. St. Agnes was at his desk again. Finally, she bade him a subdued good night and went to bed. She was asleep when he retired not long after her.

In the night, she woke suddenly, not sure what had awakened her. Then she heard it again, the too near call of a wolf. She put out her hand, but the place beside her was empty.

"Teddy?"

From the gun cabinet, he answered her. He was fully dressed, his heavy outer clothing on the floor beside him. As she hurried out of the bed and came to him. He was loading the rifle, snapping cartridges with practiced speed, levering the action with a skill that seemed all the more shocking for the deadly ease with which he moved. He looked larger than life, tough, and totally unknowable.

She stammered as she spoke, "Teddy, what is it? Where are you going?"

"Max is gone again. I was careless. I was about to wake you. That damn moose is about, and I think that pack of wolves is after it. If Max has gone with them, he could be hurt. I'm going to see if I can find him before it is too late. Will you be afraid? You're quite safe, or I wouldn't leave you."

A thousand useless thoughts crowded here mind: *Take me with you! If only I could go with you, I would see no harm came to you! Let even Max go if there's danger to you! You are my life! I can't bear to let you go! Don't go! Don't go!*

"Only for you," she said steadily. "Be very careful, Teddy."

He shrugged into his thick coat, dropped a box of ammunition in a pocket, and caught up a flashlight and his rifle.

"I shall be. You will stay inside until I come back. If Max has gone very far, it may take a while and you must not go outside. I want your promise, Jenny."

But if he were gone too long, if he could be hurt—

"I promise, Teddy." She would not have him divided in his concerns.

He was ready to go. Then his eyes swept over her huddled form, and he set everything down and took her in his arms. She pressed against him as his hands soothed down the length of her back, holding her hard against him as though he could never let her go. She clung to him in return, taking in his warm familiar scent and feeling his heart beat against her own. She thought he touched his lips to her hair. For long moments that were all too short he held her to him and then slowly put her away.

"I must go, Jenny."

"Be careful, Teddy," she said again.

"Yes," he said briefly and was gone. The sound of the door closing seemed to stay in the room a long time.

She went quickly to the window but lost sight of him almost at once. There was no moon, and the night was dark. The snow had stopped but a few flakes still swirled like moths in the edge of the porch light. It grew quiet and still with only the murmur of the fire and the clock to fill the room. She realized she was holding her breath.

The remainder of the night was endless. She sat by the fire until restlessness drove her to her feet. She roamed the cabin then, seeking reassurance. She sat at his desk, running her hands over the arms of his chair, straightening his papers out of his careful disorder into certain chaos and precisely aligning his pens. In the kitchen, she prepared coffee for the making and set out Max's marmalade. Then lest she had tempted fate with her preparations, she undid it all, slamming the refrigerator and cabinet doors shut.

In the bathroom, she found the shirt he had discarded tossed on the hamper, and she hurried into it, buttoning his scent about her. Time after time, she stood in the door listening to the muffled silence, straining to hear what was not there.

Nerves screaming, she lay down on his side of the bed, burying her face in his pillow to shut out the terrible pictures in her mind until at last she fell into a fretful sleep for an hour or more. She came awake, panicked, and sure he had come to harm for her unfaithfulness and unable to be at all reasonable. She sat then until the thin dawn began to tremble at the edge of the night, an unceasing prayer wheel circling in her mind.

He came at last in the late morning, a subdued Max trotting by his side, the moose gone and the wolves with it on a long run that was to end with the pack's objective realized. She saw at once he was exhausted; there was blood from an unexplained cut near his mouth, and the fatigue in his face was a shadow as dark as his beard. He drew her briefly into his arms, and she clung a moment in helpless relief and gratitude to the God who had heard and answered her prayers.

Then she urged him to a seat by the fire. He shed his heavy coat, his movements weary beyond measure, and she knelt against his protests to take off his boots. He went into the bathroom, and when he came out in pajama pants, she almost guided him to the bed.

He was asleep at once. Max slept already by the fire and left alone, relief took the last of her own endurance. She stood by the bed to assure herself he was really there, touching him only with her heart, and then went to sleep herself on the couch, leaving him to rest undisturbed.

When Max awoke her midafternoon, St. Agnes still slept. She took the dog out, apprehensive, but he showed no inclination to leave, and she sensed he would not again. When she had fed and watered him, he settled himself against her couch and went back to sleep.

She had a bath and wrapped in a towel went to sit by the bed as she combed out her hair. It was bright and clear outside, a hard-looking cold, the sky intensely blue and distant. St. Agnes slept and she studied his every feature as she coaxed balky tangles from her hair. She was so deeply thankful for his safe return. The long night had shown her as nothing else how foolish her reluctance, her fears. If there were to be pain and disappointment, there was also the certainty of their love. Nothing else mattered, nothing else would ever matter. When he awoke, she would explain that to him.

If only he would awake.

He moved but he was only turning in his sleep, throwing an arm over his head and pushing deeper into his pillow. Even asleep, he looked tough and powerful and as unknowable as he had in his heavy clothing the night before holding the rifle so familiarly. But she knew this man, and she wanted to be in his arms.

As any woman, she felt the need to prepare herself for her bridegroom and never had she felt more acutely the lack of feminine accessories: no perfumes, no alluring gown. Only herself. She laid the towel aside.

When he awoke, she was both shadowed and revealed by sunlight, and looking at him from the doorway. He pushed back the tangled bedcovers and stood up, looking at her in return.

She spoke his name and quite deliberately stepped toward him. He held out his arms then and she was home.

ABOUT THE AUTHOR

I have always been an avid reader. After reading lots of romance books, I decided to try writing one of my own. I hope you enjoy reading about the characters as much as I enjoyed writing about them. I live on a tree farm with my three cats.